GHOST IN THE GRAVEYARD

An AudioCraft Publishing, Inc. book

This book is a work of fiction. Names, places, characters and incidents are used fictitiously, or are products of the author's very active imagination.

Book storage and warehouses provided by Chillermania!©
Indian River, Michigan

ISBN 13-digit: 978-1-893699-16-8

Librarians/Media Specialists:
PCIP/MARC records available **free of charge** at
www.americanchillers.com

Printed in USA

Dickinson Press, Inc., Grand Rapids, MI, USA - Job 3743100 July 2010

Other books by Johnathan Rand:

Michigan Chillers:

#1: Mayhem on Mackinac Island
#2: Terror Stalks Traverse City
#3: Poltergeists of Petoskey
#4: Aliens Attack Alpena
#5: Gargoyles of Gaylord
#6: Strange Spirits of St. Ignace
#7: Kreepy Klowns of Kalamazoo
#8: Dinosaurs Destroy Detroit
#9: Sinister Spiders of Saginaw
#10: Mackinaw City Mummies
#11: Great Lakes Ghost Ship
#12: AuSable Alligators
#13: Gruesome Ghouls of Grand Rapids
#14: Bionic Bats of Bay City

American Chillers:

#1: The Michigan Mega-Monsters
#2: Ogres of Ohio
#3: Florida Fog Phantoms
#4: New York Ninjas
#5: Terrible Tractors of Texas
#6: Invisible Iguanas of Illinois
#7: Wisconsin Werewolves
#8: Minnesota Mall Mannequins
#9: Iron Insects Invade Indiana
#10: Missouri Madhouse
#11: Poisonous Pythons Paralyze Pennsylvania
#12: Dangerous Dolls of Delaware
#13: Virtual Vampires of Vermont
#14: Creepy Condors of California
#15: Nebraska Nightcrawlers
#16: Alien Androids Assault Arizona
#17: South Carolina Sea Creatures
#18: Washington Wax Museum
#19: North Dakota Night Dragons
#20: Mutant Mammoths of Montana
#21: Terrifying Toys of Tennessee
#22: Nuclear Jellyfish of New Jersey
#23: Wicked Velociraptors of West Virginia
#24: Haunting in New Hampshire
#25: Mississippi Megalodon
#26: Oklahoma Outbreak
#27: Kentucky Komodo Dragons
#28: Curse of the Connecticut Coyotes

Freddie Fernortner, Fearless First Grader:

#1: The Fantastic Flying Bicycle
#2: The Super-Scary Night Thingy
#3: A Haunting We Will Go
#4: Freddie's Dog Walking Service
#5: The Big Box Fort
#6: Mr. Chewy's Big Adventure
#7: The Magical Wading Pool
#8: Chipper's Crazy Carnival
#9: Attack of the Dust Bunnies from Outer Space!
#10: The Pond Monster

Adventure Club series:

#1: Ghost in the Graveyard
#2: Ghost in the Grand
#3: The Haunted Schoolhouse

For Teens:

PANDEMIA: A novel of the bird flu and the end of the world
(written with Christopher Knight)

American Chillers Double Thrillers:

Vampire Nation &
Attack of the Monster Venus Melon

Table of Contents

Illustrations by Darrin Brege

For my friends

Bigfoot Runs Amok

1

We didn't mean to send the town of Great Bear Heart into complete panic, but that's just what happened when the big footprints were discovered in the park on the shores of Puckett Lake one summer day.

Of course, we were partially to blame, if not mostly, since we were the ones who put the huge tracks there in the first place.

It was just supposed to be a prank. We were just trying to get back at Norm Beeblemeyer, the reporter for the *Great Bear Heart Times.* Not a single one of us thought that it would turn into the chaotic situation it became.

The idea began with the president of the Adventure Club, Shane Mitchell. He had just called the meeting to order in our clubhouse, which sits high in an old maple tree on the other side of McArdle's farm. We used to get together in Shane's dad's garage, but after we had the fire, his father wouldn't allow us to meet there anymore. Not that we could have, anyway: the fire took out most of the garage, and almost burned down Shane's house. In the end, everything turned out for the better, anyway. The six of us in the club—Shane Mitchell, Holly O'Mara, Tony Gritter, Lyle Haywood, Dylan Bunker, and myself, Parker Smith—spent a whole week building the new clubhouse high in the branches of an enormous old tree. Even old Ralph McArdle couldn't see it, and it was on his property. The fort is almost completely hidden within the thick leaves, and from the other side of the field, you can't see it at all.

Which is a good thing, because we needed someplace that was secret. We couldn't let just *anybody* know what we were up to.

We had formed the Adventure Club out of pure desperation. Great Bear Heart, the small town where we all live, really doesn't have a lot to do. It's a great little town in Michigan on the shores of Puckett Lake, and while there's a lot of outdoorsy-type things to do like fishing, hunting, hiking and biking, that's about it. No skateboard parks, no bowling alley, and the closest movie theater is fifteen miles away in another town. The six of us had started the Adventure Club in an effort to have a little fun, and make things a bit more exciting.

And I must say this: I think we almost always succeed—because whenever we get mixed up into something, you can bet that normal everyday boredom goes right out the window.

"All right," Shane Mitchell said, holding up one hand and calling the meeting to order. He was sitting on an old blue plastic milk crate, one hand on his knees. Shane is thirteen, and the oldest member of the Adventure Club. "Wednesday's meeting of the Adventure Club is now in session. Do we have any business from last week's meeting that we need to discuss?" He looked around the room for volunteers.

Dylan Bunker hesitantly raised his chubby hand, cocking his head from side to side to see if anyone else had anything to say. Dylan is ten, and is the youngest in our group. He's got a mop of thick, fire-engine red hair that hangs over his forehead and nearly covers his eyes. Dozens of freckles dot his cheeks.

"I do," he squeaked. "I still haven't been paid back that four dollars and thirty-four cents that I loaned the club last month."

Tony Gritter let out a tired groan. Tony is twelve, and has short, wiry, blonde hair. "For crying out loud," he grumbled, shaking his head as he glared at Dylan. "The club owes all of us money. You bring this up every week.

You'll get your money when we have it."

After the fire, it had taken all of the club's money to build the new clubhouse. We even had to dip into our own savings and contribute a few extra bucks to buy lumber and other materials.

"Give it a rest, Dylan," Holly O'Mara said, pulling a lock of her brown hair away from her eyes. "We'll all get our money back soon enough."

The matter was dropped. It had been agreed last month that as soon as the club came into some money, it would pay each of us back, plus a little bit of interest, if it could be afforded. Dylan Bunker looked a little disappointed. He didn't have a lot of money—but then again, none of us did. Dylan had been hoping to get paid back by now. I guess I couldn't blame him.

On this particular day, we were all still a bit miffed at Norm Beeblemeyer, the local reporter for the town's small newspaper, the *Great Bear Heart Times.* It's a weekly paper, and Norm is the only full-time reporter. He's kind of a doofus, and no one in the club likes him much, ever since he accused Tony Gritter of waxing the windows at the community library a few weeks ago. Sure, Tony is a prankster, but he'd never do anything that would cause any damage. Norm Beeblemeyer was proven wrong, of course, but not until Tony had already been blamed and even questioned by the police. To this day, Norm still believes that all of us in the Adventure Club had something to do with the vandalism at the library—and to this day, he is wrong about it.

There are a few more reasons why we don't like Norm Beeblemeyer, too. Since there's not much excitement in or around Great Bear Heart, there isn't a lot of news to report. To dig up a story, Norm Beeblemeyer sticks his nose into everybody's business, and most of what he reports in the paper just isn't true. There are more than a few people in Great Bear Heart, including all six of us in the Adventure Club, that would like to see Norm Beeblemeyer get what's coming to him.

So, when the window-waxing incident blew over, our club voted 6-0 to somehow, some way, get back at Norm.

Which is how this whole Bigfoot thing came about.

2

The topic of discussion at our meeting had shifted from money matters to Norm Beeblemeyer, and what a creep he was. We all had devised plans to get even with him, but most of our ideas were either too far-fetched or just not practical.

"I know!" Dylan Bunker said excitedly. "Let's gather up a bunch of dog mess and wrap it up in newspapers! We'll light it on fire, set it on his front porch, and then we'll—"

"Ring the doorbell and run," Tony Gritter finished snidely, taking the wind out of Dylan's sails. He continued, tiredly explaining Dylan's idea. "Norm opens the door, stomps on the fire to put it out, and gets dog mess all over his shoes." He shook his head. "That's the oldest trick in the book. Problem is, it doesn't work, and it'll probably catch his house on fire."

Dylan Bunker pursed his lips tightly, then, just as he was about to say something, Holly O'Mara spoke up, her eyes narrowed and her jaw tense. Like Lyle and Tony, Holly is twelve, but she looks older.

"We need to do something that proves to everyone that Norm Beeblemeyer is the creep he really is," she boiled.

We went around the room, bouncing ideas around. Finally, Shane Mitchell smiled, and one side of his lip curled up, then the other. Real slow-like, like he had an idea that was growing by the second. When he grinned like that, we knew he had a winner. And usually, when Shane Mitchell had an idea, you could bet it was a pretty good one.

Shane explained that he'd been reading a lot about 'Bigfoot' sightings out west . . . mostly in Montana, Idaho and Oregon. Bigfoot was supposed to be this huge, hairy creature that roamed the forests and mountains. He said the library has a couple of books that even have pictures of the beast.

"Awww, come on Shane," Lyle Haywood sneered. "Do you really believe all of that bunk?" He adjusted his glasses, then scratched his chin. Lyle is tall . . . tall and lanky. Skinny as a rail. He's the same age as Holly

O'Mara, but man . . . Lyle Haywood should be in college, not in grade school. He's brilliant. He's also the skeptical one of the group. Lyle Haywood isn't likely to believe anything unless you can show it to him.

Shane Mitchell skewered his face into a sarcastic frown. "Of course I don't believe it," he insisted sharply, furrowing his brow. A wide, toothy smile returned to his face. "But what if, all of a sudden, there was a Bigfoot creature that roamed Puckett Lake?" His smile grew. "I bet we can make people believe it—*especially* a particular reporter from the local paper."

Hot diggity-dogs. I knew exactly what Shane was thinking.

Lyle Haywood grinned broadly, and so did I, then Holly O'Mara. Dylan Bunker hadn't yet figured out what Shane was talking about, and he had a questioning look on his face. Tony Gritter knew what Shane was thinking, because a smile began to form on his lips, too, and soon it was an all-out smug grin.

And that's how the whole mess got started.

At the next club meeting, we arrived to find a brown burlap bag on the floor with a piece of paper on it. The paper read:

WARNING! BIGFOOTS INSIDE!

DON'T OPEN TILL I GET BACK!

"He spelled it wrong," Holly O'Mara pointed out. "The word 'Bigfoots' shouldn't be plural." Holly was meticulous when it came to grammar and spelling, and her school grades showed it.

"How do you put a Bigfoot in a bag?" Dylan Bunker wondered aloud. He poked at the burlap with a pudgy finger.

"Maybe it's one of those 'just add water' deals," Lyle Haywood smirked.

"Yeah," I said, chuckling. "Maybe they super-sized a 'Smallfoot' for another thirty cents."

Just then, Shane Mitchell's head popped up through the trap door of the clubhouse. Our fort is thirty feet off the ground, and you have to climb up a long rope ladder to get inside. Once we're all here, we can pull the ladder up to keep everyone else out, should anyone happen to come upon our secret clubhouse on the edge of the field.

"Whaddya think?" Shane said, grinning as he closed the trap door beneath him.

"How can we know what to think?" Holly replied, shrugging her shoulders. "We don't even know what's in the bag."

"I'll bet it's one of those 'just add water' Bigfoots, isn't it, Shane?" Lyle offered with a toothy grin. Holly glared scornfully at him.

"Better," Shane Mitchell answered, and he wasted no time in opening up the burlap bag on the table. He pulled out two items and held them up.

Big feet. That's what they were—and I mean BIG feet! It was a pair of feet, carved carefully out of wood, complete with toes and everything. Great detail had gone into the underside of the foot, and it was complete with an arch and everything. The top of the feet were flat, and had two leather straps. They looked like big wooden snowshoes.

"What in the world are those?" Dylan Bunker asked.

"It's Bigfoot," Shane answered, clearly proud of himself. "I carved them out of some scrap lumber I found." He put the feet on the ground and demonstrated how they would work.

"See? You put your feet here like this," he explained, bending over and reaching for his feet, "then you buckle these two straps around your shoes like this. That's all there is to it."

The huge feet were secured tightly to his shoes, and Shane began to walk, taking giant strides. He looked like he had two big skateboards strapped to his feet—minus the wheels, of course. "All we have to do is take these out to the park and walk around in some of the real mushy parts," he continued. "I've already tried them by my house. They work great, and leave gigantic footprints on the ground!"

"That's cool!" Dylan Bunker exclaimed.

Lyle Haywood had a sneaky grin on his face, and Tony Gritter watched, his arms crossed. Holly O'Mara leaned forward on her milk crate, watching Shane suspiciously.

Shane clomped awkwardly around the wood floor of our clubhouse. He looked a bit silly as he plodded over the oak planks, but it was easy to see how his plan might work.

Tony Gritter was unconvinced. "So, we make big tracks in the swamp," he stated as Shane came to a stop in the middle of the room. "Then what?"

"Then we write a letter to the paper," Holly O'Mara proclaimed.

Shane snapped his fingers, pointed at Holly, and nodded his head excitedly. "That's exactly it!" he agreed, smiling at Holly and then at the rest of us around the room. "We write an anonymous letter to the paper, and tell them that some strange, ape-like creature has been spotted in the park near Puckett Lake. Of course, Norm Beeblemeyer will be the one to go investigate."

"When he does, he'll find the Bigfoot tracks!" Lyle Haywood interjected, slapping his hands together.

"He'll think it's a real creature!" I exclaimed.

Our faces lit up. It would be a great prank to pull on Norm Beeblemeyer, but, more importantly, it would feel good to get him back for being such a jerk to Tony Gritter.

Of course, we didn't think about what we would do *after* Norm Beeblemeyer went to investigate . . . but one thing was for certain: we didn't expect things to get out of hand the way they did.

The *Great Bear Heart Times* is published once a week, and delivered on Friday. Which means that we'd have to give Norm Beeblemeyer a couple days head-start if we wanted him to investigate the Bigfoot tracks in the park, and have something appear in Friday's paper. We all met at the clubhouse on Monday morning and carefully crafted a note. On a plain piece of paper, Holly O'Mara wrote:

To whom it may concern:

I know this might sound crazy, but yesterday on my morning walk I saw a very strange sight. It was a large creature that looked like an ape.

It stood about eight feet tall and had hair all over its body. My, was I frightened! I rushed to tell my husband, but by the time we returned, the creature had disappeared into the forest. My husband wandered about a bit, and says that there are large footprints all over the place. I just thought someone should know. I'm not going to leave my name, because I know that you'll probably think my husband and I are both crazy. But there's something out there, I tell you. There's something in the forest, and I'm terrified. Someone should do something.

Signed,
Frightened in Great Bear Heart

We all read the note after she finished.

"You really think Norm Beeblemeyer will believe it?" I asked.

Shane Mitchell nodded. "He'll believe it, Parker," he assured. "Norm is just too nosy. He's always searching for some crazy story to dig up, and this will give him just what he's looking for. He's just *dying* to discover something like this."

Holly folded up the letter, put it in an envelope, and gave it to Dylan Bunker to run down to the post office.

"He'll get that note tomorrow," Shane said, "so we have some work to do. Tonight. Let's meet behind the library just after dark."

5

The Great Bear Heart library used to be an old train depot. The gray building sits right in front of Puckett Park, which, of course, is right on the shores of Puckett Lake. I was the first to get there, then Dylan Bunker, then Holly O'Mara, followed by Shane Mitchell and Tony Gritter. Lyle Haywood was the last to arrive.

We couldn't have picked a better night if we tried. There was no moon, and it was kind of chilly for a summer night, so there weren't any other people around. The air smelled of freshly-mowed lawns, and held a hint of wood smoke—someone, a few houses down from the park, was having a bonfire.

But what really helped us out was the fact that a thunderstorm had rolled through earlier in the evening, leaving the ground wet, soft and muddy. The tracks would be easy to make, and easy to see in the soft earth. Conditions were *perfect*.

Tony Gritter was elected to be the one to wear the big feet, simply because he has longer legs than any of us. He could take much bigger strides—even bigger strides than Lyle Haywood—and could keep the footprints a few feet apart, making the creature seem big, and all the more menacing.

Which is about what you would expect from a giant, eight-foot hairy Bigfoot that was running amok in the forest around Great Bear Heart.

Holly and I stood watch near the library, and Dylan minded his post down by the water. Lyle Haywood was the lookout from the Great Bear Heart Market, and he had one of our two-way radios. Shane had the other one, and he remained a short distance from Tony Gritter, who would be making the tracks in and around the park. Lyle was in a good place to see cars going by, or people approaching. If he thought that someone was coming, he would radio Shane, and the two could high-tail it into the woods before anyone spotted them.

Everything seemed to be going as planned. For a short time, all was quiet, and Holly and I remained as silent as we could, waiting, waiting . . . and waiting some more. We knew that, at that very moment, Tony Gritter was stomping through the dark park with the huge feet attached to his shoes. We couldn't see him, of course. All we could do was wait, and the anticipation was nerve-racking.

Twenty minutes later, I could hear excited whispering in the darkness as the two dark shapes of Shane Mitchell and Tony Gritter rushed toward us. Tony was carrying the enormous feet under his arm.

"Perfect!" Shane whispered loudly, his voice giddy

with excitement.

"That's gonna be awesome!" Tony Gritter bragged.

"What do the footprints look like?" Holly asked.

"It's too dark to tell for sure," Shane answered, "but I think we pulled it off. I've got to believe that they look great! I can't wait till Norm Beeblemeyer gets that letter!"

Dylan Bunker wanted to come back in the morning to see what the big footprints looked like, but Shane disagreed. "Someone might see us," he said. "We can't be seen anywhere near those footprints, or else someone might suspect us later on. Let's just wait until Norm Beeblemeyer gets that letter. We have to be patient."

The next day, at exactly two forty-two in the afternoon, the phone rang at my house. It was Holly O'Mara. Her voice was overflowing with excitement.

"Parker! You've got to come and see this!" she exclaimed.

"What?" I asked. "See what?"

"Down by the lake! Get down here! We're meeting at the hardware store in ten minutes!"

Things were about to go bonkers.

6

I expected to see Norm Beeblemeyer's car parked near the library, and maybe Norm trudging around the park with his camera.

What I *didn't* expect to see were the police cars and TV camera crews crammed in the small parking lot. There were dozens of people scurrying about, carrying cameras, clip-boards and notepads, looking all official-like. A yellow and black ribbon had been strung around the perimeter of the park, and uniformed police officers stood guard about every twenty feet. Police lights were flashing, groups of people were talking, and there were lots of arms pointing toward the park. It was utter madness.

Holly O'Mara was already in front of the hardware store, and I arrived at the same time as Dylan Bunker. Lyle and Tony rode up on their mountain bikes, and Shane Mitchell showed up a few minutes later, sprinting up to us, his face beat red from huffing and puffing. He had a smile on his face a mile wide.

"We did it!" he panted. "It worked! We really did it!"

"Just what did we do?" Holly asked nervously.

"We fooled Norm Beeblemeyer!" Shane replied, still gasping for air. "He bought into it hook, line, and sinker!"

"I think we fooled more people than just Norm Beeblemeyer," Lyle Haywood smirked, gazing at Puckett Park.

We all stared at the buzz of activity across the street. A TV crew was interviewing Norm Beeblemeyer, but we couldn't hear what he was saying. A policeman was talking to a few concerned residents that had gathered at the side of the road. A press conference was in session at one of the park picnic tables. A man wearing a black suit and a red tie was answering questions.

Tony Gritter and I were nominated to casually mosey on over to see what we could find out. We skipped across the highway and slipped innocently into the crowd of people.

The parking lot was so packed with people and vehicles that it was difficult to even walk through. Cars were parked only a few inches apart, but we managed to squeak by and make it down to the park.

I recognized Officer Hulburt, standing by a towering oak tree. He and my dad are friends, and had gone to school together. Officer Hulburt is pretty cool. He was the one who helped us out when Norm Beeblemeyer accused Tony Gritter of waxing the windows of the library. He saw us walking through the park, and we walked over to where he stood.

"Hey guys," he smiled warmly, waving as we approached.

"Hi, Officer Hulburt," I replied, looking around at the confusion. "What's going on?"

Officer Hulburt shook his head, and a big smile came to his face. He looked like he was about to let us in on some big secret. "It's the craziest thing," he grinned, his cheeks glowing. "There are some strange footprints all around the park. Big ones. Like from some big creature or something. Far too big to be made by any human. Norm Beeblemeyer says he found them this morning."

"You don't say?!?!" I replied, trying to sound and look astonished. Inside, I was bursting with laughter. I know Tony was, too.

"Yeah, they're really something to see," Officer Hulbert whistled. "I can't let you back there right now, otherwise I'd let you guys go see for yourselves. They're bringing up some expert from the university to examine them later this afternoon."

My heart sank as I heard those words. An examiner from the university would surely discover that the giant footprints in the mud were phony, and then the jig would be up.

Rats.

"Well, what do they think it is?" Tony asked harmlessly.

"Beats me," Officer Hulburt shrugged, "but they say it looks like some big creature that walks upright on two legs. Like those Bigfoot creatures that are supposed to live out west. If you believe in those things, anyway."

We said good-bye to officer Hulburt and walked back across the street to where Shane, Lyle, Holly, and Dylan were waiting. Their eyes were glued to all the excitement.

"It's working!" Tony Gritter snickered as we approached. He gave the 'thumbs up' signal, and his smile broadened. "They really think some kind of creature made those prints!"

"Of course they do," Lyle Haywood replied, matter-of-factly. "That's how we planned it."

"I just wish we could've been here to see Norm Beeblemeyer's face when he saw those tracks," Holly O'Mara confessed. "That sure would have been funny."

Across the street, the bustle of activity continued. Townspeople had gathered around the sidewalk in small clusters, talking about the mysterious creature that had made the huge footprints in the park. Ed Skinner, the town Mayor, was busy hustling from one group to the next, trying to pick up more and more bits of information. Lucy Marbles, better known as the town gossip, was doing the same, only she was making much more of an effort than Mayor Skinner. Lucy Marbles was a meddlesome, ornery woman with a penchant for sticking her nose where it didn't belong. She also had the benefit of a wild imagination, and I'm sure the Bigfoot story grew and grew with every person she spoke with.

But sadly, we knew that it would all be over later today. When the specialist from the university arrived, he would quickly determine that the footprints were fakes.

Oh well. It was kind of fun while it lasted. The tiny town of Great Bear Heart was at last seeing a bit of action, courtesy of the Adventure Club.

Of course, we didn't know it at the time, but the real fun was just about to begin.

7

The town of Great Bear Heart is named after an old Potowatami Indian Chief who lived here in the 1800s. Great Bear Heart, the town, is like a lot of other small towns in America: down-home folks who all pretty much know one another, people who look out for their neighbors. There are two churches, a post office and a township building, a hardware store, a bar and grill called *Rollers*, a market with gas pumps, a library, a thrift store, and a small restaurant called *The Kona.* A single, paved, two lane highway goes through the middle of the town. There is also a network of blacktop roads that weave in and around a few small subdivisions. All in all, there are only several hundred people who live in Great Bear Heart.

But when gossip goes wild in Great Bear Heart—and

often it does—it has a way of taking on a mind of its own.

By evening, Lucy Marbles had spread the rumor that dogs and cats had suddenly been missing around town, and she claimed the 'experts' were saying that Bigfoot could be responsible. At least this was the story that Lucy circulated. It was, of course, entirely untrue. She hadn't talked with any 'experts' any more than she had talked with a little man from Mars. But her pet story scared townsfolk into bringing in their dogs and cats from outside. Even Mayor Skinner, who has a goat, decided to bring the animal in for the night. I can't imagine a goat running around inside Mayor Skinner's house, and I know for a fact that Mrs. Skinner was pretty hot about the whole deal.

No one wanted to take any chances, though. After all, a dangerous, eight-foot, hairy creature was on the loose in Great Bear Heart.

Word got out that the expert from the university had arrived, and that there would be a press conference in the parking lot of Puckett Park at eight o'clock. We all raced down there after dinner to hear the bad news broken.

The park was still filled with police cars and trucks, and two more TV stations had arrived. A large crowd had already started to gather, and people chattered among themselves in small groups. A microphone and speaker system had been set up, so that the growing swarm of residents would be able to hear what was being said.

"Don't you think that maybe we ought to keep a low profile?" I asked Shane. "After all, when they announce that this whole thing is a big fraud, Norm Beeblemeyer is going to suspect us right off the bat."

Shane shook his head. "I doubt it. And even if he does suspect us, he can't prove a thing."

At ten minutes past eight, an older, bespectacled man took the stage, holding a stack of papers in one hand, and a huge, white plaster cast of a footprint in the other. He had a scowl on his face and a stern look in his eyes. It was obvious that he was probably upset at the fact of being called all the way here, only to find that the whole thing had been a practical joke.

He leaned toward the microphone, and spoke.

"Ladies and Gentlemen," he began. His voice was rough, deep, and very serious. "Upon careful study of this rather extraordinary find, I am absolutely convinced that—"

The microphone suddenly went dead. His mouth continued to move, but we were too far away to hear what he was saying. Suddenly, a crewman from one of the television stations leapt forward, fiddled with some wires, and got the microphone working again.

"—as I was saying," the man began again. "This finding is truly one of monumental importance in the history of anthropology. These tracks, in my opinion, are indeed *genuine.*" He glanced at the plaster cast, and held it out for the crowd to see. "I believe that whatever made this footprint is still out here somewhere." He raised one arm and waved it slowly, as if denoting the forests around the small town.

A low gasp surged through the crowd of spectators, followed by a dramatic hush. A wave of fear washed over the spectators. The six of us just stared, mouths wide.

"I have seen many fakes in my life," the expert continued, "and these, ladies and gentlemen, are definitely *not* fakes. I, for one, believe they were made by an unknown creature. A creature that many people have come to call 'Bigfoot'."

The crowd went wild. Newspaper people were busy scratching things down on notepads or typing furiously into laptop computers. Portable phones appeared out of nowhere, and the chattering reached a dull roar.

"Yes!" Tony Gritter softly hissed. He doubled his right hand into a fist and pounded the air. His smile was wide, and his eyes were on fire. *"It worked! It really worked!"*

The rest of us were too dumbstruck to say anything. We just watched the hordes of people rushing frantically about. Hands flew up in the air, questions were shouted. Still other people began devising plans to capture the great beast alive. More people ran home to make sure that their pets were safe indoors, thanks to the story made up by Lucy Marbles. The six of us stood silently beneath the awning of the hardware store, watching.

Finally, Holly O'Mara spoke up. "Now what?" she asked, posing the question to club president Shane Mitchell.

It was a good question. I guess we all just figured that Norm Beeblemeyer would maybe take some photos of the footprints and put them in the paper, and later on we could somehow call his bluff, and everybody in town would realize that Norm had been had. None of us expected that the whole thing would get blown out of proportion like this. I think that some of us were even a bit worried. I know I was.

But not Shane Mitchell. He had his infamous smirk that told us that he'd thought up another plan.

And I must admit, this one was bound to be one of his better ones.

8

Shane called for an early meeting the very next morning, and we all gathered at the clubhouse at eight, sharp. We were all on time except for Dylan Bunker, who arrived his typical fifteen minutes late.

"Okay, what's up?" Lyle Haywood asked Shane. Shane wouldn't tell us last night what he'd planned, but wanted to wait until this morning. We were all anxious to find out what he had up his sleeve.

"How much money is the club in the hole for?" Shane asked Holly. Holly O'Mara recited the number from memory, which is one of the reasons why she makes such a good club treasurer. She looked up at the ceiling, as if drawing the numbers from the air.

"Including all of the money that the club owes each of

us, and the ten dollars that Lyle Haywood borrowed from his dad, the club owes forty seven dollars and twenty eight cents."

"Suppose," Shane began, "we can pay all of that back today, and even make enough to have a surplus in our coffee can?" Our coffee can was where we kept the club money. It was stashed under a log in the woods not far from the clubhouse.

We all stared at Shane. We couldn't figure out where he was going with this one.

"Okay, here's the situation," he continued. He leaned forward on the milk crate and folded his hands. His eyes drifted to each one of us as he spoke. "There's going to be lots of people down at the park today, right?" We all nodded our heads. There was sure to be a ton of people pouring into Great Bear Heart. "Scads of people are going to be looking for that creature," Shane continued, his eyes burning with excitement. "There's only one restaurant in town, and one market. The restaurant is too small to feed all those people, and the market will be jammed all day long."

Lyle Haywood began to smile. The rest of us still didn't figure what he was getting at just yet.

"What I'm saying," Shane Mitchell continued, the smile on his face growing, "is that the Adventure Club

Roadside Diner is now open for business."

9

By nine-thirty there was already a good crowd of people milling about Puckett Park. By ten, the single highway through town was nearly at a standstill. Cars, filled with gawkers and sightseers, crept along like snails, all hoping to get a glimpse at the mysterious beast.

And by ten-thirty, the Adventure Club Roadside Diner had officially opened.

We had three card tables lined up, and we placed two big pieces of plywood in front of them. Holly and I took orders for cold beverages, while Tony Gritter grilled hot dogs and hamburgers on a small gas grill set up behind us. The grill belonged to Shane Mitchell's mom and dad, and he'd managed to somehow sneak it from their deck and wheel it down the hill to the park without his parents knowing about it.

Lyle Haywood made a big wood sign to advertise. He'd come up with some clever names, too. We had 'Bigfoot Burgers' and 'Carnivore Corn Dogs.' The hamburgers and corn dogs came from Holly O'Mara's house, but we ran out pretty fast. Which was okay, because we'd already made enough money to run across to the market and buy more hamburger ourselves. George Bloomer, the owner of the market, was glad to see our operation in full swing. He said his small store couldn't handle all of the business anyway, so we weren't taking any sales away from him by putting up a stand across from his store. In fact, he said that he'd sold more hamburger meat to us in one morning than he usually sells all week, so he was glad for our business.

Our beverages were hot sellers as well. Lyle called the Lemonade 'Monster Juice'. He'd originally called our iced-tea 'Bigfoot Blood' . . . but, with a name like that, we didn't sell much, as you can imagine why. It just sounded *too* gross. When he changed the name to 'Sasquatch Quencher', we sold oodles of the stuff. Marketing, as they say, is *everything.*

Our customers were anyone and everyone. Thirsty townspeople gulped down the lemonade by the gallon. Television crews would send one of their workers over to order for their colleagues, and some of them ordered eight or ten burgers at a time. We were so busy that Shane Mitchell took over grilling duties for a while so Lyle Haywood could go find another grill. He wound up sneaking one from his own house, just like Shane Mitchell had done.

"Carnivore Corn Dogs!" Dylan Bunker hawked. "Get your Carnivore Corn Dogs, just one dollar!"

"Monster Juice, just seventy-five cents!" Holly O'Mara chirped.

A line began to form at all three tables, and we couldn't serve our customers fast enough. The money just kept rolling in.

In short, the Adventure Club Roadside Diner was a smash success. By noon, the club had made enough money to pay each of us back. By three o'clock, we'd cleared nearly seventy-five dollars, and that was *after* expenses. George Bloomer finally let us charge the food items we needed, and we agreed to pay our bill at the end of the day.

By seven o'clock that evening, business had slowed down considerably. We called it quits for the day, paid George Bloomer what we owed his store, and met back at the clubhouse. Holly counted up the money and divided up what was owed to each of us. Dylan Bunker was overjoyed. After everyone was paid back, we'd cleared one hundred thirty-three dollars and six cents! Not only had we been able to pay everyone back, but we had some money in our coffee can to boot. I went to bed that night with dollar signs in my eyes. We'd made a ton of money—and the next day would be even better.

Or so we thought.

10

We'd planned to get the Adventure Club Roadside Diner started at ten o'clock the next morning—*but someone else beat us to it!*

When I saw the stand already set up in front of the park, I'd figured that Shane and Lyle arrived early to get things set up. But when I got closer, I realized that they weren't our tables at all.

Someone had swiped our spot!

Not only that, but they'd put up their own sign . . . in the exact same spot we'd had ours the day before! They called their stand the 'Creature Cafe'. They were selling hot dogs and hamburgers, and lemonade and iced-tea, just like we had done yesterday!

Instantly, I knew who it was.

The Martin brothers. All three of them, to be exact. Terry, Gary, and Larry. We should have expected it. If there's anyone who would do such a thing, it would be them. They've given all of us trouble for a long time, and we have a sneaking suspicion that they were the ones who waxed the windows at the library. In fact, all three of them were, at one time, Boy Scouts. All three were kicked out within a year for disobedience. They missed meetings, didn't follow directions, and broke just about every rule the Scouts had. None of them had even bothered to try and earn any merit badges, and only Gary progressed passed the rank of Tenderfoot. All three Martin brothers were jerks, plain and simple.

I kept my distance and hung out at the hardware store, watching the roadside stand. Holly O'Mara finally showed up, and she, too, was dumbfounded when she saw the Martin's stand across the street.

"What . . . what in the world is going on?!?!?" she stammered.

I couldn't answer her. I just shook my head.

After a few more minutes, the rest of the club arrived. Shane, Tony, Lyle, Dylan, Holly, and I stood under the awning of the hardware store, watching the Martin brothers. Not one of us said a thing.

The situation looked grim. We couldn't put up another

stand right next to the Martin's. I mean, I guess we could, but we'd certainly make a lot less money than we did the day before.

It wasn't fair. The Martin brothers had stolen our idea.

And to make matters worse, every once in a while, Terry, who was the oldest of the brothers, would look over at all of us and brandish a sarcastic smile . . . usually right after he'd sold another hamburger or hot dog.

Shane called an emergency meeting at the clubhouse in an hour, exactly. He said that he'd need some time to set up a few things. What those 'things' were, he wouldn't say. He said that we'd know soon enough.

In exactly one hour, we were all at the clubhouse, except for Dylan, who was fifteen minutes late, as usual.

Shane called the meeting to order without Dylan, and he didn't waste any time in issuing directives.

"Tony," he ordered, "you and Lyle go set up the roadside stand across from *Lazy Shores Resort.*" *Lazy Shores Resort* was a small resort on the shores of Puckett Lake, about a quarter of a mile south of the park. There were eight separate cabins, all placed alongside one another. It was pretty busy all summer long, as it was the only place of its kind in Great Bear Heart. The cabins were rented to vacationing tourists.

"But that's a long ways away from anyone!" Holly

pleaded. "The people are down at the park!"

Just then, Dylan popped his head through the trap door.

"Sorry I'm late, guys," he apologized, scrambling through the floor and taking his usual seat against the wall.

"Dylan," Shane Mitchell commanded, as though Dylan had been there all along, "you'll help me load up my Dad's golf cart down at the market."

A lot of people have golf carts in Great Bear Heart. Since the town is so small, lots of folks use golf carts, instead of cars, to run their errands.

Shane looked at Holly O'Mara. "Holly, you go with Lyle and Tony and get the Monster Juice and Sasquatch Quencher ready. Those coolers will be heavy, and they'll need all the help they can get." He looked at me. "Parker, I need you to make an important phone call."

"But Shane," Tony interjected, "there's hardly anyone down at *Lazy Shores Resort*. Like Holly said—they're all down at the park!"

Shane flashed a confident smile, and we all hoped he knew what he was doing. "Not for long, they won't be," was all he said. "Not for long."

11

Shane had given me careful instructions. I waited at my house until he called, then I hung up, picked the phone back up again—and dialed the number to the local radio station.

I told them that my name was Arnie Zarshaken, and that I had just spotted a giant, ape-like creature in the woods—right across from *Lazy Shores Resort.* I hung up, hopped on my bike, and high-tailed it to meet Shane Mitchell downtown.

Dylan and Shane were at the hardware store, perched on the seats of their mountain bikes, watching the huge crowd in the park. They had just returned from the stand that Holly, Tony, and Lyle were setting up across from *Lazy Shores Resort.*

The Martin brothers were doing a great business.

There were two lines of people waiting to get served. I was still hopping mad about how they had stolen our idea. They had stolen our idea—*and* our customers.

Things were about to change.

Suddenly, people began running to their cars! Just like we'd hoped, the radio station had contacted their crew at Puckett Park, telling them that the creature had been spotted a quarter of a mile away . . . near *Lazy Shores Resort!*

Car engines roared, and vehicles spun out of the parking lot. People that were waiting in line at the food stand suddenly bolted in every direction. There was so much confusion that one of the cars bumped into one of the tables where the Martin brothers were selling food, and ten gallons of lemonade tipped over in one giant gush, splattering all over the gravel shoulder. Larry tried to save the huge cooler before it went over, but he only succeeded in knocking over two full tins of hamburgers that had yet to be cooked. The meat tumbled into the gravel and dirt. A little black dog that was scampering through the park caught wind of the upended burgers, and began hungrily gobbling them up. Gary Martin looked comical chasing the little dog around the park, trying to keep the furry thief from eating the meat.

It was chaotic. TV crews hurriedly packed up their gear and sped off. Police cars, sirens blaring, roared away from the scene.

Satisfied, Shane looked at his watch.

"Right on time!" he exclaimed urgently. "Let's go!"

Loose dirt spun beneath our bicycle tires. We were off, pedaling like mad down the shoulder of the road.

In seconds, we were in front of *Lazy Shores Resort*, where a large crowd was already growing. Most of the people that had been down at the park were now swarming the area around *Lazy Shores Resort.* Everyone was on the lookout for Bigfoot.

Shane's plan had been simple, and it worked like a charm. In the hour before the meeting that he needed to 'set things up' he had sneaked into the woods adjacent to *Lazy Shores Resort.* He plodded around with the big feet strapped to his shoes, making big imprints in the ground near the lake and along a small creek. I, of course, didn't see them, but Shane said that the footprints looked awesome—and, after my phone call to the radio station, it didn't take long for someone to find them.

"Over here!" we heard an unseen voice shout. Frantic scrambling ensued as people began dashing through the woods. Branches snapped and cracked as hoards of people thundered through the woods. A police megaphone barked orders for people to stay back, that the creature could be dangerous. The only thing that they found, obviously, were tracks from the beast, but there were a few nervous moments as people looked behind thick brush piles to see if the creature had gone into hiding. One of the police officers, fearful that the creature could be near, drew his gun as a precaution.

It took about a half an hour for the initial excitement to wear off, and for things to get busy at our roadside stand. At first, people were more interested in seeing the large tracks in the mud than they were in eating food, so business was slow. But as news leaked out, more and more people showed up, clogging the highway and slowing traffic to a standstill. Soon, hundreds of people were combing the area around *Lazy Shores Resort.*

And our business skyrocketed.

12

Later that night at our meeting, we counted up the money. One hundred seventy-seven dollars and forty-eight cents! That gave us a grand total of three hundred ten dollars and fifty-four cents for both days! I had never seen so much money.

The local paper, the *Great Bear Heart Times*, printed their weekly edition early because of the sensation. Lyle Haywood brought a copy to the meeting. A picture of the beast's footprint was on the front page, along with a picture of Norm Beeblemeyer—and boy, was Norm full of himself. He stated in his story that he'd been investigating the strange creature for weeks, and that he had actually spotted the creature in the hills just beyond Great Bear Heart.

"That's a flat-out lie!" Tony Gritter flared angrily.

"He's making it all up!"

Norm Beeblemeyer had gone on to write that *he* had been the one to discover the huge prints in the park, after his 'weeks upon weeks of scouring the forest'. He made no mention of the letter he had received—the letter *we* had made up and sent him!

"He's hogging all of the attention himself!" I fumed. "That's not fair!"

"Relax," Shane Mitchell said, trying to cool things off. "That's just what we want, isn't it? Let him have his fifteen minutes of fame. This whole thing will backfire on him somehow. You watch."

Shane was wrong . . . because things weren't quite about to backfire for Norm Beeblemeyer.

Oh, they were about to backfire, all right—on us.

The next day, a coincidental chain of events occurred that can only be described as 'bizarre'. They began with a frantic phone call from Shane Mitchell to Tony Gritter. It was just past eight in the morning.

"Tony! The feet! They're gone!" His voice was flooded with panic.

"What are you talking about?!?!" Tony asked groggily. The phone call had awoken him from a sound sleep.

"I went to get them out of the garage this morning, but they're gone!" Shane explained. "The only thing there is an empty bag!"

This sounded the alarm, and we held yet another emergency meeting at the clubhouse. We were all talking and trying to figure out what had happened to the feet. Dylan Bunker was his usual fifteen minutes late, but this time we heard him coming from across the field and up the rope ladder. He was running at full bore—something Dylan Bunker never did. Dylan is usually so slow that if he moved any faster, he'd be going backwards.

He burst through the floor all out of breath, huffing and puffing like a sick dragon.

"What's up with you?" Lyle Haywood asked as Dylan collapsed in a heap on the clubhouse floor.

"Tracks," he gasped in between giant gulps of air. His cheeks were red and puffy from running so hard. "There are tracks—Bigfoot tracks—*all over town!"*

"What?!?!" Shane exclaimed. "Did you see them?!?!"

Dylan nodded his head. "Yep! And man, they're *everywhere!"*

This was a disaster. Bigfoot tracks around town meant two things: first, someone had obviously stolen our wooden Bigfoot feet, but most importantly, someone knew that we were behind the whole thing! We'd been found out!

"Okay, okay, let's keep a clear head about his," Tony Gritter reasoned. "So, someone's got our big feet. All we have to do is find out who."

"I'll bet it's the Martin brothers," Holly O'Mara said coldly. Her cheeks were flushed in anger, and she clenched her teeth. "I'll bet they're behind this."

"That doesn't make sense, though," Shane replied. "They had no idea what we were up to. Even if they did, those feet were hidden away in a burlap bag. They would have never found them."

By the time the six of us high-tailed it to town, the mood was frantic. Just like Dylan said, there were Bigfoot tracks everywhere. People scrambled all over the village, snapping pictures, pointing, trying to find out where the huge creature had been and where he might be headed.

Suddenly, Shane Mitchell's face turned white. His mouth opened, and his eyes popped right out of his head.

"The Martin brothers weren't behind this!" he exclaimed, slapping a palm to his forehead. "I'll bet you a buffalo nickel that it was my kid brother! He's a nosy little bugger! I'll bet he was playing in the garage and found the feet! Oh Man! Why didn't I think of that in the first place?!?!"

We were in a jam. If Shane's little brother was indeed the culprit, it meant that, sooner or later, he would be heading home . . . with Bigfoot tracks winding all the way up to Shane's house!

"Come on!" Lyle Haywood shouted. "We've got to make it back to Shane's house before anyone else does!"

We were off. To make things a bit less conspicuous, we all left in different directions, circling the neighborhood, in case Shane's little brother wasn't headed for home. Shane would head straight back to his house, while the rest of us split up and took different routes.

True to Shane's suspicions, we found tracks heading up to his house. His little brother must have taken the feet early in the morning. While we had been holding our emergency meeting, the little thief was running around town creating havoc. It was amazing that he hadn't been spotted by someone already.

But we knew it was only a matter of time. There were other people hot on the trail as well. They were following the footprints . . . and it wasn't going to take them long to find out where the tracks were headed.

13

I took off on my bike and headed around to the back of Shane's house, so I would come in from a totally different direction than everyone else. There are a lot of trails that wind through the woods around neighborhood, and we all know them like the backs of our hands. I hoped I could make it without being seen and arousing any suspicion.

Coming up behind Shane's house, I stashed my bike in the brush and scouted out the area. There was no sign of anyone yet . . . *except Ryan, Shane's little brother!*

Oh no!

He was coming up the driveway, with the enormous feet strapped to his shoes! His steps were clumsy and difficult. Ryan is seven years old . . . the wooden feet were far too big for him to be walking with, but he was managing, somehow.

And he looked like he was having the time of his life! Every couple of steps he would stop, turn around, look at the footprints he had just made, and giggle.

Step, step, stop, giggle. Step, step, stop, giggle. Ryan was having a blast.

There was no time to lose.

"Ryan!" I shouted, sprinting across the yard. I ran as fast as my legs would carry me. Surprised, Ryan stopped where he was, staring at me. I ran up to him.

"Ryan, I need you to do a favor for me. Can you go down to the market and get me a candy bar?" I stuffed my hand into my pocket and pulled out a dollar. "If you do, you can buy one for yourself. Free. But I need you to hurry, so you'll have to leave those big feet here."

I didn't have to ask him twice. He stared at the dollar in my hand, then reached down and unsnapped the huge feet from his shoes. In a flash, he was off. The whole exchange took ten seconds.

I had to act fast. I was certain that there were people following the tracks Ryan had made. They would be here any second.

But I had a plan.

Without wasting another moment, I buckled the wooden feet to my shoes and took off across the yard in a near run. It was pretty hard going with those huge feet strapped to my sneakers, but I managed. I was careful to pick every soft spot in the ground that I could. I wanted to make sure that whoever was following the tracks would be able to find them easily.

I skirted the house and snuck off into the woods—and not a moment too soon. I heard a car coming, and I turned to see a police cruiser moving slowly along the driveway, along with a few people walking slowly next to it! They were all staring at the ground, following the tracks. Flashbulbs were popping, and people were looking anxiously around. They knew they were getting close to Bigfoot.

There's a small stream in the woods not too far from Shane's house, and I headed for it. I sure hoped my idea would work! If I could pull it off, we could wrap up this whole thing without anyone being the wiser. Granted, it was a pretty daring plan, but at the time it seemed like my only option. In fact, the only other option at the time was to get caught—in the act.

No way, I thought, as I lumbered through the forest with the big feet strapped to my shoes. Branches smacked my head, and twice I almost fell.

At the creek, I turned and followed it downstream, making sure my tracks were visible in the black muck. I wanted to be certain that the people following me wouldn't lose my trail.

The creek winds south of town, passes just beyond the *Lazy Shores Resort,* goes under the highway, and then flows into Puckett Lake. My plan was to follow the creek down to the lake and weave my way back to the park, where the tracks would get lost among all of the other tracks.

If I wasn't spotted, anyway.

I could hear branches crunching and breaking behind me, and I knew that the Bigfoot hunters weren't far off. I was glad that they hadn't brought any dogs along! I'd be a goner, for sure.

But as I sloshed along through the mud next to the creek, I also began to realize that there was no way I was going to make it back to the park. My pursuers were too close. I was going to be caught red-handed!

I trudged on. I wound around and behind *Lazy Shores Resort,* keeping an eye out for anyone that might spot me. I did see a few people, but they seemed distracted by other things that were going on across the street.

I had to think fast. I was pretty much out in the open, and I could be spotted real easy. It's hard to miss a thirteen-year-old with small canoes on his feet.

Think. *Think.*

I was standing near the edge of the forest, frantically

wondering what to do, listening to the breaking branches and twigs in the forest behind me. The pursuers were coming closer, and in a few minutes they would be coming through the brush.

Then, I spotted Norm Beeblemeyer's parked car.

14

In five minutes, the noisy group of searchers emerged from the forest. They were tense and their heads turned as they stepped out into the open, for they knew that they were closing in on the dangerous Bigfoot creature.

I was standing at our roadside stand, getting things ready for the day, sipping on a glass of Monster Juice. Moments after the Bigfoot search party had emerged from the forest, Holly O'Mara came speeding up on her bike, followed by Lyle Haywood. Shane Mitchell wasn't far behind, followed by Tony Gritter and Dylan Bunker. I wore a grin from ear to ear, and I acted like I hadn't a care in the world.

"Parker! What's going on?!?" Holly asked, leaning her bike against a tree and running up to me.

I just smiled. Shane, Tony, Dylan and Lyle all rushed up to the stand.

"Don't look so nervous, guys," I coaxed. "Relax. Just pretend that nothing's going on."

The group of searchers hastily crossed the highway and picked up the huge tracks once again, following them through the dirt, around a mostly-dried mud puddle—and right up to the passenger door of Norm Beeblemeyer's car.

"Parker, you didn't!" Shane exclaimed in disbelief. His eyes never left the growing group of people next to Norm Beeblemeyer's car.

"I did," I smirked.

The group around Norm's car began to get noisy and loud, and we could tell they were thoroughly disgusted. Someone opened up the car door and pulled out two very large wooden feet—and held them up for the gathering crowd to see.

15

Norm Beeblemeyer had a lot of explaining to do. Of course, everyone knew that he hadn't been the one who had led the group on the goose chase, since he was with the party of searchers that had followed the tracks through the woods and along the stream and back to his car. But everyone figured that somehow, Norm was in on the whole scheme, even though they couldn't prove it.

The next week's paper printed an apology and a retraction from Norm, saying that he'd been 'caught up in all the excitement' and that he had been 'carried away'. He adamantly insisted that he didn't have anything to do with the Bigfoot tracks, but not many people believed him. He'd been caught with the wooden feet in his car. Norm Beeblemeyer had egg all over his face, and there were at least six people in the town of Great Bear Heart that thought he got exactly what was coming to him.

At our next meeting, we spent the first half hour talking about the Bigfoot adventure. Dylan had a copy of the paper, and we took turns reading it out loud, giggling to ourselves.

"Serves him right!" Tony Gritter exclaimed, after reading Norm's apology in the paper.

We all laughed about it for a while, and thought that the whole Bigfoot episode would be the most fun we'd have all summer.

That is, of course, until the day Lyle Haywood found the old, beat-up submarine in Alfred Franklin's junkyard.

Project: Submarine

1

Lyle Haywood was late for the meeting. Not just late, but *really* late. That's not like him at all. Dylan Bunker, always about fifteen minutes late, was even there before Lyle. We all speculated where he might possibly be, but we were at a loss. Lyle Haywood is probably the most prompt member of the Adventure Club. This just wasn't like him.

Holly O'Mara was in favor of starting the meeting without him, but Shane Mitchell shook his head.

"Nope," he said, looking out the open window of the clubhouse. He stared down through the dark clusters of maple leaves that hid our clubhouse high in the branches of the huge tree. Our clubhouse has windows, but they're open, without any glass or screen. In the summer the maple tree is thick with dark green, palm-sized leaves that hide the clubhouse well.

"We wait," Shane continued. "He'll be here. He'll—"

He stopped speaking, and leaned closer toward the window, peering intensely through the dense foliage.

"—he's here," he finished smartly, with a hint of satisfaction in his voice.

Soon, we all could hear the telltale swishing of grass, the *thump-thump-thump* of sneakers on dirt. Lyle was running, and pretty fast at that. The galloping grew louder, closer, then stopped abruptly, some thirty feet below us. Lyle's groans and grunts could be heard as he whisked up the rope ladder. Lyle only weighs about eighty pounds completely soaked, even though he is almost as tall as Shane. He's pretty handy at climbing up the rope ladder.

Suddenly, the trap door in the floor snapped open, and Lyle's hand appeared. His head popped through the square opening.

"Nice of you to make it," Tony Gritter said sarcastically.

Lyle Haywood ignored Tony's comment. He was out of breath, and when he pulled himself up through the door and closed it, he collapsed to the floor, sitting cross-legged and leaning forward.

"You guys aren't gonna believe what I found," he panted, looking around the room. He raised one hand to his face and adjusted his glasses with a single finger.

"Your watch?" Holly O'Mara jibed, smiling.

Lyle Haywood shook his head. "A submarine!" he exclaimed, spreading his arms wide. "A *real* submarine! Over in old man Franklin's junkyard!"

Alfred Franklin was pushing eighty-five years of age. He's got a crop of thick, white hair and a full beard and mustache. In many ways, he looks like Santa Claus, only Mr. Franklin is quite a bit thinner. Since 1948, he's owned the only junkyard in Great Bear Heart. It's located out of town about a half-mile, and not too far from Lyle's house. Whenever we needed spare parts for this or that, Franklin's junkyard was the place to go. And he always gave us a good deal on stuff, too. I guess he figured that, because we were kids, none of us had much money, which was true. We always got whatever we needed pretty cheap from old Mr. Franklin.

"Slow down, slow down," Shane Mitchell told Lyle. "You found a *what?*"

"A submarine!" Lyle answered proudly, once again adjusting the glasses on the bridge of his nose. He was relaxing, and he was breathing easier now. His face was alive with excitement.

"Get outta here!" Tony Gritter said in disbelief.

"What would a submarine be doing in a junkyard?"

Dylan Bunker pondered.

"Are you sure it's a submarine?" I asked. I couldn't imagine why something like that would be in Franklin's junkyard, or how it would even get there in the first place.

"Honest!" Lyle said. He raised one hand in pledge. "I was looking for a piece of steel that I could use to make a fishing rod holder for my dad's boat. Way in the back, past all of the old cars and trucks that are piled up, I saw this thing that looked like a big, iron tube. As big as a pickup truck! I walked all around it and checked it out."

"So, what makes you think it's a submarine?" Shane quizzed. "And what would a submarine be doing in Franklin's junkyard?"

"I asked old man Franklin the same thing," Lyle answered, his voice growing with excitement. "He said that the submarine was an old research vessel that some college had once used. When it got old, the college had no place to put it. So Mr. Franklin said that they could drop it off in his junkyard if they gave him two hundred dollars. The engines are in really bad shape and she's got a lot of rust, but—"

Lyle stopped speaking, and he looked at every one of us. His eyes went from Shane, then to Holly, then to me, over to Tony, then to Dylan Bunker. "—but I think we can make it work," Lyle finished. Behind his glasses his eyes were shining like sunlight on chrome, and he looked like he was under some sort of spell.

Holly O'Mara frowned. Dylan Bunker groaned. Tony Gritter's face was expressionless, still sizing up the situation. Shane Mitchell's forehead was all squished together, like he was deep in thought. I myself had serious doubts. To be sure, a submarine *did* sound like a lot of fun, but it just didn't seem practical.

We were all silent for a moment. Finally, Shane spoke up.

"Nope," he said, shaking his head. "It's a great idea. But it would cost too much. We'd drain—"

Lyle Haywood was shaking his head, causing Shane to stop in mid-sentence.

"All of the work could be done in my dad's boathouse down at the lake," Lyle insisted. "The engines, all of the rust . . . it can all be fixed. My dad's got an awesome set of tools, and we can use whatever we need."

"Yeah, but we would have to buy the sub from old man Franklin," I said. "It'll cost us a fortune. Where are we going to get the money?"

"Maybe we could set up another diner on the road!" Dylan Bunker mused excitedly. "We could sell submarine dogs and torpedo weenies!"

Again, Lyle Haywood shook his head, only this time,

there was an even bigger smile on his face. "It's already taken care of," he said confidently.

We all looked at him incredulously.

"Just what do you mean by 'it's already taken care of'?" Holly asked.

"My dad plows the snow from Mr. Franklin's driveway all winter long," Lyle explained. "Dad never takes any money from him. When I was asking about the submarine, Mr. Franklin said that he would give it to us, for *free*, as kind of a 'thank-you' for all of Dad's plowing. But we have to promise not to bring it back. I guess he's had the thing for a while and no one wants it. He says it's just cluttering up his junkyard, if you can imagine that." Lyle looked around the room anxiously. "So . . . I told him we'd take it."

And it was that simple. We took a vote, and, of course, we all voted in favor of re-building the submarine. Especially since we didn't have to buy it. I was a little skeptical from the start, thinking there was no way that we could get an old research submarine to work again. After all, re-building a submarine isn't like re-building a bicycle, or even re-building a car, for that matter. I was sure that it wouldn't be watertight, or we wouldn't be able to get the engines working, or we'd never be able to find replacement parts. I was certain that the thing would sink on its first test-run.

I was wrong.

2

By far, the submarine project was going to be one of the most challenging endeavors that our club had ever taken up. We estimated that the sub weighed about a thousand pounds, and it was no small job to move it. Holly O'Mara's older brother has a big flatbed truck that he uses for hauling construction equipment, and he helped us out. Mr. Franklin has a heavy-duty winch that he used to lift the sub onto the back of the flatbed. Holly's brother drove it carefully down to the lake, and then we had to use the hoist in the boathouse to get the thing off the truck. It took all day just to get the old sub from the junkyard to the boathouse.

The arrangement worked well, however. We left the sub in the hoist and worked on the vessel in the boathouse, which was cool because we could close the doors to keep anyone—especially the Martin brothers—from knowing what we were doing.

One thing was for certain: we sure had our work cut out for us.

Tony Gritter and I got to work repairing the steel hull. Tony's dad taught him how to weld a few years ago, and he's become pretty good at it. I pedaled my bike back and forth to Franklin's junkyard, bringing back pieces of flat metal and steel for Tony. He welded the plates to the hull, and, although it didn't look real pretty, Tony was sure his patch job would keep the water out.

Shane Mitchell and Lyle Haywood worked on the engines, and Holly O'Mara and Dylan Bunker got to work on the inside of the sub, repairing the old controls and replacing the two seats. Dylan can be kind of a klutz, but he took his job seriously and worked hard. And while this was all new to Holly O'Mara, she's brilliant when it comes to figuring things out in her head. She and Dylan worked well together, and the cockpit of the sub soon began to look pretty cool. There were only two seats, but there was a good-sized space behind them where the rest of us could sit or kneel. The interior of the submarine would be cramped, but we'd be able to fit all six of us inside.

We worked through the entire month of June. There sure was a lot to learn about submarines. We had to learn about pressurization, compression, oxygen storage, and all kinds of things that you don't really think about at first. I read piles of books on submarines and how they work, and so did everyone else in the club.

The work was tedious, difficult, and slow. There were so many gadgets and gizmos and pumps and things, and they all had to work *perfect.* When we weren't actually

working on the sub, all of us had our noses in books, going over plans and details and information.

Finally, at four-thirty in the afternoon on July 3rd,

Shane and Lyle finished working on the motors.

The submarine was finished.

"Let's take'er out tonight!" Dylan Bunker said, his voice alive with enthusiasm.

But Shane disagreed. "Nope," he said, shaking his head. He wiped away a bead of sweat that dribbled down his nose. "We'll lower the sub into the water tonight, but we'll let it set till tomorrow. We'll have all night to see if it's watertight. That way, if any leaks develop, we'll catch them before our initial test run."

Lowering the sub into the water proved to be a difficult task in itself. The sub weighed a lot more than a boat, and we had to go slow. It took us over an hour to lower the sub into the water trough in the boathouse, but we managed.

Most of the vessel was submerged below the surface, and only the main hatch was visible. Lyle Haywood closed the two wooden doors of the boathouse, hiding the submarine from view. He bolted and locked the doors, and we all went home.

Although none of us could wait to try out the submarine, we'd have to. Shane was right, as usual. For safety's sake, we needed to be sure that the ship was watertight. We'd know in the morning if the submarine had developed any leaks.

But I had a hard time sleeping that night.

3

I got up at five-thirty the next morning, sprang out of bed, and got dressed. I grabbed two *Pop-Tarts* and wolfed them down cold as I hurried down to the lake. I was determined to be the first one to the boathouse.

Not so. Dylan Bunker was already there, sleeping next to a tree. I snuck up on him, and surprised him when I arrived.

“Boo!” I said, shaking his shoulder. He jumped to his feet, eyes wide. He looked like he’d seen a ghost. When he saw that it was only me, he relaxed.

“Did you stay here all night?” I asked.

He shook his head. “No,” he replied, yawning. “But I got here pretty early. I couldn’t sleep, so I walked down here.”

"Looks like you were doing a pretty good job of sleeping a minute ago," I said, grinning.

A crack of sunlight was slowly growing on the far side of the lake, giving way to a slate-gray sky. The early morning air was cool and fresh, and unseen birds began to sing high in the trees. The weather had been great for the past week, and no rain was in the forecast for a few more days. It was going to be a *perfect* fourth of July in Great Bear Heart.

Shane Mitchell arrived a few minutes after myself, followed by Holly O'Mara. Tony and Lyle were the last to arrive, both riding up together on their bikes.

At the boathouse, Lyle unlocked the two big doors, and Shane and Holly swung them open.

"Well, let's find out if we're going to take the old beast for a spin," Shane said. He knelt down on the dock, opened the hatch of the submarine, and popped his head into the dark hole.

It was the moment of truth.

"This is kind of like groundhog day," Tony Gritter snickered. He raised his voice. "Hey Shane . . . I hope you don't see your shadow when you pop your head out of there. Otherwise, we'll have six more weeks of repairs to the sub."

"Funny, Tony, real funny." Shane's voice echoed,

hollow and booming, inside of the vessel. "You're a regular comedian."

We were all silent for a moment. I could see Shane's head turning from side to side. If he stretched his neck down any farther, I was sure he'd fall right into the sub.

"Looks like," he reported, his voice echoing through the sub. Shane raised his head and looked at us, and the smile on his face said it all. He stood up and rubbed the palms of his hands together. "Looks like we're going for a ride," he finished.

We let out a cheer. None of us could contain our excitement. Dylan Bunker was doing a silly dance on the dock, and I thought he was going to wet his pants.

"We have to pick a name," Holly O'Mara said. "Before a ship sets sail, it has to have a name. We have to christen it."

We hadn't thought of that.

Since Lyle Haywood was the one who found the sub, we decided that it would be up to him to choose a name.

"Don't pick something dorky," Tony Gritter warned.

Lyle Haywood stood on the dock, deep in thought. He stroked his chin, and squinted as he looked at the submarine. The sun was rising higher, and the day was warming. A few early morning boats had appeared way out on the lake.

Finally, Lyle smiled, and adjusted his glasses with his pinky. "Well," he said, "it *is* the fourth of July. How about we call'er *Independence?*"

"Perfect!" I exclaimed.

"Yeah, that's great!" Dylan Bunker shouted.

"That sounds cool!" Holly O'Mara agreed.

"Then it's settled," Shane Mitchell said approvingly. "*Independence* it is!"

And that was that. We lined up on the dock in sort of a salute, and Lyle pulled out his pocket knife and unfolded the blade. Crouching down on the dock, he held the knife like a sword and touched the blade to the dark metal of the sub.

"As a member of the Adventure Club, I christen you the *Independence,*" he said proudly.

"Here, here!" we all shouted, slapping high-fives among ourselves.

It was the fourth of July, and we were about to set sail.

4

It was pretty cramped inside the sub. The air was cool and heavy, with a faint, stale odor of oil and grease. Lyle Haywood and Shane Mitchell sat in the cockpit, where they could man the controls. The rest of us were squished in behind them.

"Close the hatch, Holly," Shane ordered. Holly reached up and pulled the heavy steel disc closed. With a few twists of the air lock wheel, she had secured the hatch.

The front of the sub was one big, rounded window, and the only light in the vessel came from beneath the surface of the lake. We could see really good, and I must say that I've never seen anything quite like it. It was like we were looking into a big aquarium. A small bluegill and several rock bass darted right in front of the window, inches from the thick glass. Pea-green seaweed carpeted the bottom of the lake, and we could see dozens of mussels and snails. It was awesome.

"Whoah," Lyle Haywood gasped. "This is too cool."

"Let's fire up the engines," Shane said. He flicked a couple switches, and, after a few clicks and churns of the motors, the sub roared to life. The engines coughed and sputtered at first, then smoothed out to a steady hum.

"Everybody ready?" Shane barked over the drone of the engines.

"Ready!" I answered.

"Let's go!" Dylan Bunker chimed in.

"Yeah, let's!" Holly O'Mara urged.

"Nah, I'm kinda bored," Tony jested. "Let's go knit a sweater." I shook my head and laughed, and gave Tony a gentle punch in the shoulder. Tony just smiled. He was just as excited as anyone to take the sub for its very first run.

Lyle grasped a shift lever with his right hand, and he gently pushed it forward. There was a loud *thunk* as the engines slipped into gear, and the whole ship shuddered. The submarine suddenly lurched and chugged—and began to move forward.

I could feel the excitement boiling in the sub, but not one of us said a word. The air was electric.

Lyle piloted the vessel close to the lake bottom, and we could look up and see the shiny surface above. It was awesome.

"We're at twenty feet, Captain Mitchell," Lyle reported smartly.

"Thank you, Captain Haywood," Shane Mitchell replied, real official-like. "Carry on, and continue at present speed."

Independence crept beneath along the bottom of Puckett Lake, and every second was more thrilling than the last. We saw dozens of fish—some big ones, too.

"Check that out!" Dylan Bunker suddenly blurted out, pointing over Shane's shoulder. We all hunched forward, peering over and around one another to see what he was looking at.

A northern pike, nearly four feet long, cruised directly in front of us. Pike are long, tube like fish, and they are probably the most vicious creatures in the lake. They are kind of a seaweed-green color under water, and they have white bar-like spots on their sides and on their backs. Pike have razor-sharp teeth, and they eat just about anything and everything they can fit into their powerful jaws.

As the huge fish passed, Lyle turned the sub and began to follow it. The pike seemed wary, but Lyle was able to keep pace, staying a few feet behind the fish. After a few moments it became spooked, and it took off with a single, explosive swish of its powerful tail.

Right then, there was no place else I wanted to be. Video games and television now seemed so . . . so *boring*. And dull. This was where the *real* fun was. This was what the Adventure Club was all about.

As Lyle piloted the *Independence* deeper and deeper, the water around us grew dim. The surface high above us was a dark, milky gray.

"How deep are we?" Dylan asked.

"Fifty-six feet, Captain Bunker," Lyle replied. Dylan giggled quietly. I think he liked being addressed as 'Captain'. I think we all did.

Below us, the lake bottom was thick and bushy, covered with aquatic plants of all kinds. Some of the plants were long and stringy, and grew straight up like thin, green spaghetti. Others were dense and leafy, and grew in tight clusters on the bottom like burly tumbleweeds. Minnows darted among the plants, and alarmed crayfish backed away, claws raised in warning, as the submarine drifted past. The whole experience was breathtaking.

A large log came into view below us, and the sub slowly glided above it.

Oh, there wasn't too much exciting about cruising over a submerged log, as we'd already came across a few of them. Years ago, Puckett Lake was used by lumbermen to carry timber through the inland waterway, and many logs became waterlogged and sank to the bottom. A few of them were huge . . . two feet in diameter, and as long as a car. Some were smaller, and rotting away. All were covered with a half-inch film of greenish-brown sludge from years of submersion.

So when the *Independence* passed over the big log, we thought nothing of it.

Until the log began to move.

5

"Holy smokes!" Shane Mitchell suddenly exclaimed. Holly O'Mara screamed. Dylan Bunker screamed, too, and he placed his hands over his face, covering his eyes. I didn't scream, but when the log moved, it surprised me so much that I jumped and hit my head on the top of the sub.

"Check that out!" Lyle declared. "It's a sturgeon!"

And it was! A *huge* one. A sturgeon is a fish—a prehistoric fish, at that—that have been around for millions of years. It was about six feet long, and a dark, dirty gray color. The top of his tail was longer than the bottom part, and it slowly swished back and forth as the enormous fish lumbered on. We all relaxed a little as the huge beast began to slowly swim off. He'd given us all quite a start. Some sturgeons get really big, like the one we were watching right now. There are a few of them in Puckett Lake, but they are shy, and you don't see them very often.

It was incredible. Seeing the massive fish, as close as he was, was extraordinary. The sturgeon was bigger than we were, and probably heavier, too. We all knew that what

we were seeing was a once-in-a-lifetime thing, and watching the fish filled us with awe and wonder.

"Let's follow him," Lyle Haywood said, gently easing the controls. The *Independence* slowly turned to the left, and we began to stalk the huge fish as he cruised above the weeds below us.

"This is too cool," Holly O'Mara whispered.

Although we were moving, time seemed to stand still. The fish below us was truly one of the most unbelievable sights I had ever seen. Sure, we'd all seen things like this on TV and video, but to see it for real—to really *experience* it first-hand—was dazzling. I can't remember ever feeling so awed and amazed at the world around us. These creatures are alive and around us in Puckett Lake, every single day. Seeing the mammoth-sized sturgeon so close was simply magnificent.

"Did anyone bring a camera?" Tony Gritter asked.

"Aw, man, that's what we forgot!" Shane Mitchell complained, slapping his palm to his forehead. "I thought about that last night, too! Man! I can't believe I forgot it!"

The sturgeon continued to glide sluggishly above the weed beds. If he noticed us, it certainly didn't seem to bother him much. The fish just took its time, lazily swimming along.

"Seventy-seven feet," Lyle said, glancing down at the gauges, then returning his gaze to the immense fish below us. "We're really deep."

The waters around us grew dark and murky. The deeper we went, the harder it was for the sunlight to penetrate through. When I looked up, I couldn't even see the surface anymore. There was just a drab, gray, flat sky that loomed overhead. It was an eerie feeling.

But suddenly, something strange happened. As we followed the sturgeon, the waters in front of us grew *very* dark. It was as if night had fallen. In a moment, we found out why.

"It's an underwater tunnel," Shane Mitchell whispered breathlessly.

We all watched silently as the huge sturgeon continued along, finally disappearing into the wide, black opening of the tunnel.

"Quick! Hit the lights!" Lyle Haywood exclaimed. "Let's see if we can see where he goes!"

One of the things that Tony Gritter added on to the *Independence* were two rotating spotlights that could be controlled from inside the sub. He used a small electric motor from the driver's side rear-view mirror of a car (a 1976 Ford Granada) that he found in Franklin's junkyard. It was a stroke of genius on his part, and the lights worked great.

Tony hit the switch. The beams of light shot out from the sub like lasers, illuminating the inside of the tunnel. The fish was nowhere to be found, but by now, we'd forgotten about it. We were spellbound by the wide, dark tunnel that seemed to go on and on, forever.

Using the mounted remote control, Tony swung the spotlight beams around the outside wall of the mouth of the tunnel. It looked like it was solid rock.

The shafts of light swung back into the tunnel, and Tony slowly moved the bright beams back and forth. Lyle had slowed the submarine to a stop a few feet off the bottom of the lake. We hovered in one spot, several yards from the entrance of the tunnel.

"I know what everybody's thinking," Shane Mitchell said quietly. And he did. He knew exactly what we were thinking at that moment.

We were all thinking about exploring the tunnel.

Shane turned and glanced at each of us. "You want to vote on it?"

"I say yes!" Dylan Bunker exclaimed, raising his hand. I nodded my head in agreement, and so did Tony Gritter.

"Are you sure we should try it?" Holly O'Mara asked. "I mean . . . it might be dangerous."

"We'll be fine," Lyle Haywood assured. "We'll just be really careful."

Silence filled the cabin. Then:

"Okay," Holly agreed, with a tone of apprehension in her voice. "I vote yes. I vote we check it out."

And that was that. With a couple of quick adjustments

and a gentle nudge of the controls, the *Independence* slowly began to move forward. What little light we had been surrounded by quickly vanished. The only thing we could see was the sweeping, white blades of the spotlights as the submarine entered the mysterious tunnel.

6

"Careful," Shane said. "Go slow."

It was a really weird feeling, being so deep in the water, yet surrounded by rock walls. In some places, the beam of light illuminated sharp, jagged rocks that stuck way out into the tunnel. If we hit one of those, we'd be goners.

"Geez," Dylan Bunker wondered aloud. "How far does this thing go?"

"Well, so far we've gone about a mile," Shane Mitchell said, after a quick check of the gauges. "And my guess is that it goes all the way to Lake Huron."

All the way to Lake Huron!?!?!? That would be cool! Puckett Lake is part of a chain of lakes that connect through various rivers and streams. The entire water system flows into Lake Huron, one of Michigan's Great Lakes. And when they named it a 'Great' lake, they weren't kidding! Lake Huron is one of the largest bodies of fresh water in the world. It's more like a small ocean than a lake. If Shane was right, we'd be in Lake Huron soon.

But not before Lyle realized something.

"Whoah, man!" he suddenly whispered, glancing down at the gauges. *"We're two hundred feet deep!"*

It seemed unbelievable. The tunnel must've slowly sloped downward . . . so gradually that we didn't notice it.

And then, without warning, the walls around us disappeared. One second the walls were there, and the next—gone. We were in complete darkness. It was a very strange feeling.

"Where . . . where are we?" Dylan Bunker stammered.

"It's Lake Huron!" Shane replied ecstatically. "It has to be! We're in Lake Huron!"

"Only one way to find out for sure," Lyle said, flicking a couple of switches. "Let's surface. We need to freshen our air supply, anyway."

Lyle and Shane made a few adjustments. We could feel the submarine begin to rise, and the bow slowly sloped upward. I grabbed the back of Lyle's seat so I wouldn't fall backward. But in the darkness in front of us, it didn't look like we were moving at all. All we could see were two white beams piercing the inky black waters. It was kind of weird.

But soon, a foggy, gray cast began to appear above us.

"Getting there," Shane Mitchell said, looking up. "Take'er nice and easy."

The gray cast grew lighter and lighter. Then, we could make out waves and ripples, and curtains of light streaming the blue-green waters. Within a few seconds the *Independence* surfaced, and we could hear waves lapping against the steel hull.

"Tony, open up the hatch and see where we are," Shane ordered. "Lyle . . . fire up the compressor and fill our tanks with some fresh air."

I didn't know too much about how the air compression system worked, but Shane had explained that it was like a big scuba tank. It stored all of our air, so we could stay under water for a long time. An exhaust system circulated the oxygen, and eliminated what was already used up.

Lyle flipped a switch, and the compressor buzzed to life. Tony unscrewed the pressure-lock and flipped the heavy steel hatch door open. Fresh, clean air swirled down into the *Independence*. Warm sunshine splashed inside, illuminating the inside of the sub. We all squinted in the bright light. Tony scrambled up and popped his head out.

"HOLY COW!" he suddenly screamed, tumbling back

into the sub and slamming the hatch closed. He was hysterical. *"Dive! Dive!"*

"What?!?!" Shane asked loudly, alarmed by Tony's plea. "What are you talking about?!?!?"

"WE'RE IN THE MIDDLE OF THE SHIPPING LANE!" Tony squealed, frantically spinning the pressure lock wheel tight and securing the hatch. *"We surfaced in the shipping lane! A freighter is coming! It's almost on top of us!"*

7

Talk about panic! We freaked out. The *Independence* had surfaced in a shipping lane in Lake Huron, which is heavily traveled by oceangoing freighters. The ships are so big that they could run right over us, and they wouldn't even know it!

Lyle shut down the compressor and throttled up the engines.

"Hang on!" he barked. "This is going to get rough!" All at once, the *Independence* was in a steep nose-dive. Tony, Holly, Dylan and I had to hold onto one another to keep from falling into the cockpit where Shane and Lyle were. We began to plummet away from the surface, down, down, away from the speeding freighter.

Unfortunately, we weren't going to escape unscathed.

don't get the sub steady, we're done for!"

The *Independence* continued to spin madly out of control, and the six of us were tossed about the steel hull. The waters grew dark, and we knew we were sinking rapidly. Nothing Lyle did seemed to get the submarine back under control.

Things were not looking good.

A red light started blinking, and a loud beeping sound filled the sub.

Whoop . . .whoop . . .whoop . . . whoop . . . .

"We've lost power to the motors!" Lyle shouted above the screeching alarm.

The submarine steadied a bit, but we were still in an all-out dive, almost straight down. In seconds, we were so far from the surface that we were in total darkness again. The only illumination in the submarine came from the blinking red alarm light.

Dylan Bunker was sniffling, and Tony Gritter was scrunched next to me. "Ow-ow-ow-ow-ow-ow-ow," he repeated over and over.

"Are you all right?" I asked.

"Ow . . . yes," Tony replied. "I smacked my elbow on something. Ow-ow-ow-ow-ow-ow-ow-ow!"

"Quit being a baby and see if you can get the spotlights back on!" Shane Mitchell ordered from the cockpit of the sub. The spotlights had blinked out during the near-collision with the freighter. "Lyle . . . how fast are we sinking?"

"Best I can tell, we're dropping about five feet a second," Lyle said frantically. "If I . . . can't . . . get—" He was really struggling with something. "If I can't get the motors started, we're . . . going . . . to . . . slam into the bottom of . . . Lake Huron!"

For the first time in my life, I think I was *really* frightened. I've been scared before, but nothing like this. I guess that, for the first time, I realized that something really *serious* could happen to us, and there was no one around to help. We were stuck. Stuck in a steel tomb.

All of a sudden, two white beams pierced the dark water in front of us, brightening the interior of the sub. I could once again see the dark silhouettes of my friends.

"Great work!" Shane cried out from the front.

"Yeah, great!" Dylan Bunker replied anxiously. "Now we can at least *see* what we'll be smashing into!"

Shane was barking out orders, but in the confusion, it was hard to hear. The warning siren whooped loudly, and we were all talking at once.

Then, a stroke of luck came our way. The engines suddenly sputtered and choked! The vibrations of the sluggish motors shook the entire vessel.

"Come on," Lyle urged gently from the cockpit. "Almost. Almost there—"

The engines heaved one more time, then smoothed out to a steady drone. We all cheered. Lyle instantly threw the motors into reverse and we could feel the *Independence* begin to slow. It felt like riding in an elevator that was coming to a stop. I felt a surge of relief, and I knew that everyone else did, too. Lyle had control of the sub by now, and we were no longer plunging wildly toward the bottom of the lake.

And it was just in the nick of time, too . . . because in the beam of the spotlights, the bottom of Lake Huron slowly appeared. We could see the sharp, jutting edges of rocks protruding up from the lake bottom.

Not a word was spoken. We all knew how close we had come to being smashed to smithereens at the bottom of Lake Huron.

"I can't believe that almost happened," Holly O'Mara breathed.

We'd had two really close calls within a matter of seconds. First, we almost hit the freighter, and second, we almost smacked into the bottom of the lake.

But now things were looking up. The submarine hadn't sustained any real damage, and, besides a few scrapes and bruises that the six of us suffered from being tossed around in the sub, we were all okay. I don't know how, but none of us had been seriously injured.

The *Independence* cruised slowly and safely a few feet from the bottom of Lake Huron. We all breathed easier, thankful that we had averted disaster.

"Enough adventure for one day," Shane Mitchell said with a sigh of relief. "Let's head back to someplace safer."

"I second that," Dylan Bunker said, raising his hand. "I've got a bloody nose, and my head hurts."

"Maybe when you rang your melon, you got some sense knocked into you," Tony Gritter snapped playfully. Dylan responded by shooting Tony a dirty look.

"Holly, are you okay?" Shane Mitchell said, not taking his eyes from the front of the submarine.

"I'm fine," she answered.

"Parker? How about you?"

"Yeah, I'm okay," I replied, rubbing the back of my neck. My head pounded, but my lip had stopped bleeding. I was fine.

But, as we were to find out, our problems weren't over just yet.

9

Finding the underwater tunnel wasn't very difficult, and soon the *Independence* was creeping slowly through the dark cavern.

We were all feeling a little bit better. I have to admit: the submarine sure was fun, but that freighter really scared the daylights out of me. I would be glad when we got back to Puckett Lake. There certainly weren't any freighters to worry about there.

The return trip through the tunnel was uneventful. The walls were jagged and dark, and there wasn't much to see. Lyle Haywood was really getting good at maneuvering the *Independence,* and he guided the vessel back through the tunnel skillfully.

At last, the mouth of the cavern opened wide, and the

submarine slowly left the darkness of the underwater tunnel. The waters were a murky, greenish-gray, and we knew we had returned to Puckett Lake. Once again, we all breathed a sigh of relief. We had made it home.

Almost.

Puckett Lake is a busy place on the fourth of July. There are dozens—maybe hundreds—of boats and jet-skis that take to the water. As the *Independence* rose closer and closer to the surface, we could see occasional dark shadows speeding on the gray surface above us—boats pulling water skiers, sailboats cruising lazily across the lake. I thought it was really cool that, here we were, in the depths of Puckett Lake, and no one could see us. No one even knew we were here.

"Hey, take a look at that up there," Dylan said, pointing over my shoulder.

About twenty feet in front of us, a white line extended from the bottom of the lake to the surface. A dark shadow was buoyed above.

"Somebody's got their anchor out," Shane Mitchell said. "Must be doing some fishing."

"Wouldn't it be funny if we hooked the sub onto their lure?" Tony Gritter said devilishly. "Man . . . they would think that they've hooked onto the biggest fish in the world!"

We all laughed at that. The thought of someone on the surface trying to reel in our submarine with a fishing pole did sound funny.

"Yeah, but we'd break the line," Shane replied. "If he ever found out, he'd sure be mad at us."

Independence continued plodding along, directly beneath the fishing boat.

"We don't have very far to go now," Lyle offered, looking at the panel of gauges while he piloted the vessel. "I think we're—"

Suddenly, there was a loud *bang!* on the steel hull, and the entire sub jerked violently sideways.

"What's going on?" Dylan Bunker cried out. We all held out our hands, grasping the walls and one another to steady ourselves.

The submarine stabilized, but we still couldn't figure out what had caused the sudden noise.

"We must have hit something," Shane Mitchell speculated.

"That's impossible," Lyle Haywood disagreed, turning the *Independence* slowly around. "There was nothing there."

"Oh, yes there was," Holly O'Mara suddenly cried out. She pointed up toward the surface, and we all crouched down and gazed up to get a look.

Just below the dark shadow of the fishing boat, an anchor was rising, rapidly being pulled upward.

"How about that," Lyle chuckled. "That fishing boat is pulling up its anchor! We got hit by the anchor! Good thing it didn't hook onto us!"

Another laugh echoed through the submarine. The thought of being hooked onto an anchor, pulling the boat around, was even funnier than hooking onto the fishing lure.

The *Independence* continued to move slowly through the water. We saw a few more fish, even a couple of big pike and bass. Having our own submarine sure was cool. I thought about the fun we would have the rest of the summer with the *Independence.*

All of a sudden, I felt something cold around my feet, and I looked down. Holly O'Mara must have felt the same thing at the same time, because she looked down, too.

The elation and excitement I had been feeling immediately turned into complete horror.

"WATER!" I cried out. "We've got water in the bottom of the sub! *Independence* is leaking!"

Everyone looked down. An inch of water covered the bottom of the sub.

Shane Mitchell scrambled from the cockpit and began searching the inner hull of the sub. In a matter of seconds, he found the problem.

And it wasn't good.

10

"Right here!" Shane Mitchell said, his voice anxious and tense. "Water is pouring in like crazy! When that anchor hit us, it must've split a seam in the steel hull!"

Sure enough, a steady stream of water was quickly trickling down the side of the sub.

In the next instant there was a loud *pop!* and the seam split open even more! Water didn't just pour in . . . it sprayed in like a showerhead gone mad! In seconds, we were all soaked through our clothes.

"Surface!" Shane Mitchell screamed, turning toward Lyle in the cockpit. *"We have to get to the surface! We have to abandon ship!"*

Quickly, Lyle flipped a couple of switches and pulled on the controls. The *Independence* began to rise.

Thankfully, we were in about twenty feet of water, so we didn't have far to go.

But we were taking in water *fast.*

Lyle shot a quick glance back at me. "Parker!" he barked. "When we hit the surface, blow the hatch and get out! Jump into the water! It's our only chance! The sub is going to sink!"

"Can everybody swim?!?!?" Shane asked loudly over the spraying water. We all nodded our heads. We were all pretty good swimmers. Shane knew this, but I think hew as just double-checking.

Question was: how far were we going to have to swim?

The sub approached the surface, but just before we reached it, we began to slow down. Water continued to spray in through the wall of the sub. It was already up to my knees.

"What's wrong?" Dylan asked. "How come we're not moving?"

"I'm trying!" Lyle Haywood answered. "But were taking in a lot of water really fast! We . . . we might not make it all the way to the surface!"

Terror set in.

"We've gotta make it," Dylan Bunker whined. "I've got a ball game tonight."

"Okay, I'm going to try something," Lyle said. "Hang

on. If this works, we'll shoot right to the top. But there's so much water in the sub, I don't think we'll be there for long. We've taken in too much water already. As soon as we break the surface, get out as fast as you can!"

"Okay," I said, holding the pressure-lock wheel in both hands. "I'll open the hatch. Holly . . . you go first. Dylan, you go after Holly. Tony, you go after Dylan."

Shane turned and looked at me. "You go up after Tony," he said. "I'll be right after you."

"And I'll try and hold us as long as I can," Lyle said, still struggling with the controls. The sub was moving toward the surface, but it seemed painfully slow.

Then there was a loud *ker-klunk!* And the submarine suddenly popped right up to the surface. Whatever Lyle Haywood had done, it worked.

"Now! Now! Now!" Lyle commanded sharply. *"I can only hold her here for a few seconds!"*

Without a moment's hesitation, I twisted the pressure lock and heaved the hatch open. Light streamed in—bright and glorious, warm and beautiful. I squinted in the blazing sun. A few seconds before, I didn't think I'd ever see sunlight again.

"Go, Holly!" I shouted. "Hurry!"

Holly O'Mara pulled herself up, and I gave her a push as she crawled out the hatch. She disappeared, and we heard a splash. She'd made it.

Dylan was next, and he sloshed his way through the spraying water in the sub. He had a bit more difficulty than Holly, but in a moment, he, too, had splashed into the open water.

"Tony! Go!" I shouted, and Tony Gritter blasted out of the open hatch like a rocket. No need to tell him twice!

I was next, and I shot an anxious glance back at Lyle and Shane.

"Go!" Shane ordered, scrambling from the cockpit. "Hurry! We're going to sink! *Independence* is going down!"

I spun and raised my hands in front of my face to stop the spray of water from hitting me in the eyes. The split in the seam of the hull had grown, and water gushed in with the force of a geyser. The water in the sub was now up to my knees. We were taking in water rapidly.

In one quick movement, I pulled myself up and through the hatch, rolled over the steel hull, and splashed down into the water. Holly, Dylan, and Tony were a few feet away, and I swam over to them. Surprisingly, we weren't very far from shore at all. Maybe a hundred feet or so. Lyle had been pretty good with his calculations. In the distance, I could see the boathouse where we'd re-built and launched the *Independence.*

There was a splash behind me, and I turned to see Shane Mitchell pop his head above water. He swam to us, stopped, and turned.

But there was no sign of Lyle.

"Lyle!" I shouted. "Lyle!"

We were all treading water, staring at the sliver of the hull that was visible. Sunlight glowed on the dark, wet steel. No sounds came from the sub.

Still no Lyle!

"Lyle!" we all began to shout. "Come on! The submarine is sinking! It's going down! Lyle!"

Without warning, the submarine lurched sideways, and water began to pour into the open hatch!

"Lyle!" Shane screamed. He began to swim toward the sub, and I followed. We swam frantically, crawling arm over arm in the water toward the doomed vessel.

All of a sudden there was a loud hiss, the awful sound of escaping air. *Independence* rolled sideways, and in one swift motion, sank beneath the surface—and vanished.

Lyle Haywood had gone down with the ship.

11

Every one of us was screaming. Lyle Haywood was gone. He hadn't been able to get out in time, and had become trapped in the submarine.

I dove beneath the surface, and to my surprise, I could see the sub as it sank. Bubbles rose from the gaping hatchway, and from the split in the hull. The stern of the vessel had already hit bottom.

And Lyle Haywood was still inside! He had saved our lives by bringing the *Independence* to the surface . . . but now he was going to lose his own!

This was worse than a nightmare. It was a catastrophe.

I frantically splashed to the surface, took a deep breath, and dove back down. Shane Mitchell had done the same, and both of us swam side by side to the sunken sub. The

Independence had only been under water for a few seconds, and it might already be too late—but we were going to do everything we could to save Lyle. He was our friend, and we had to do something.

When you open your eyes underwater, everything is blurry. But if you squint a little bit, things become a little clearer. I was squinting, searching for the hatch on the sunken sub . . . when Lyle's head suddenly popped out! He was alive! He was struggling to get out of the hatch!

He extended an arm, and Shane and I grabbed his wrist, pulling him from the opening of the submarine. Lyle was alive! He was out of the sub!

He rocketed toward the surface, and Shane and I kicked off from the bottom, following right behind him. The three of us exploded out of the water, coughing and sputtering. Lyle heaved and gasped, sputtering and choking. He'd lost his glasses, but at the moment, I don't think he really cared.

"Oh man," he choked. "Oh man! I thought I was a goner!"

"We did, too!" I sputtered. "Am I glad to see you!"

"We're all glad to see you!" Holly O'Mara exclaimed.

We all took one last look at the spot where the *Independence* had gone down. Bubbles were rising to the surface, and they boiled and popped in the hot afternoon sun.

Independence—the vessel we'd worked so long and hard to restore—was gone.

But we were alive . . . and right now, that's all that mattered.

12

We had a special meeting later that evening to discuss a few things. We'd made some really big mistakes with the whole submarine project, and we didn't want to repeat them. We hadn't taken any life preservers, which was pretty dumb, and we hadn't taken a radio, either, which was really, *really* dumb. There were other mistakes, too . . . any one of which could have got us killed. The six of us vowed to do a bit more pre-planning with any project we took upon ourselves. We wanted everyone in the Adventure Club to be around for a while.

But our undersea exploration was sure to be something that I would never forget. It was so different, so very, very cool. I'd bet that not many other kids our age have had the opportunity to re-build a submarine. I thought for sure that restoring the *Independence* and exploring the waters of Puckett Lake would be the most exciting adventure of the summer.

And it would have been, too.

But then one morning, Dylan Bunker found a hidden door behind a bookshelf in the town library.

The Hidden Door

1

Dylan Bunker certainly didn't *intend* to find the hidden door behind an old bookshelf at the Great Bear Heart Library. But when he accidentally pulled out ten books instead of two, he couldn't help but notice the curious wood door that was tucked away behind the shelf, camouflaged from view.

Strange, he thought, peering between the books at the dusty old door. *What's that doing back there?*

He'd been at the library for an hour, looking through the collection of *Hardy Boys* mysteries, trying to find *#28: The Sign of the Crooked Arrow.* The book seemed to have disappeared, and it was the only one in the series that Dylan hadn't read. Mrs. Norberg, the librarian, said that it hadn't been checked out recently, but she was sure that it was there when she'd completed her yearly inventory last winter. Dylan Bunker was certain that the book was gone forever, and it was driving him nuts.

After finding the door, Dylan had called each of us on the phone, requesting an emergency meeting. He didn't say why. When he'd called me, his voice was brimming with excitement, like it was his birthday. He said he was on to something big—he just didn't know what.

Of course, most of us thought that an old door in the library wasn't really important, and certainly not something the Adventure Club would be interested in.

Not yet, anyway. That would come later.

Now, he was seated high up in our clubhouse on a blue plastic milk crate, eyes wide, telling us what he'd discovered.

"Tell us again," Shane Mitchell said with a bit of impatience in his voice, "just what the door looks like, and how you found it."

"Well," he began, "it's like I said. I was pulling a book from the shelf, and a bunch of other books came with it. They fell all over the floor, and made an awful racket. When I went to put them back, I noticed the door." His eyes grew even bigger as he recalled the incident. "It's made out of wood, and the door handle has been broken off. But there's a small skeleton-key hole. The kind of keyholes you see in old doors."

"What did Mrs. Norberg say about it?" Tony Gritter asked disinterestedly. He was seated in the corner of our clubhouse, chewing on a long piece of grass.

Dylan shook his head. "I didn't tell her," he said, "just in case I wasn't supposed to know it was there."

"It's probably just a storage room," Lyle Haywood said, his arms folded in disdain. He had wanted to go fishing with his dad that evening, and the emergency meeting had put his plans on hold.

A heavy wind was blowing, gently rocking the clubhouse to and fro. The boards creaked and moaned with every shift of the evening breeze.

"I think Lyle's right," I said, nodding my head toward Lyle Haywood, but looking at Dylan. "I think that it's probably just some place where they store books or something."

"But guys," Dylan protested, spreading his arms and looking around the room at each of us, "why would the door handle be broken off?"

"Maybe it was an accident," Shane Mitchell said, shaking his head a bit and raising his hands to show both palms. "That old building was built back in the eighteen-hundreds. It's bound to start falling apart sooner or later."

We were coming down pretty hard on Dylan, probably

a little too much. While Dylan Bunker wasn't the sharpest knife in the drawer, he had a heart of gold, and he was a true friend. He was really excited about finding the door, and thought that all of us would be, too. I was feeling a little sorry for him. Holly O'Mara was too, and she came to his defense. Up until now, she'd sat quietly on a wooden crate, listening. Now, she spoke up.

"I think we should check it out," she proposed. "I mean . . . maybe it's nothing. But maybe—"

We all looked at her, waiting for her to finish her sentence.

"—maybe there's something to it. Maybe there's some secret room or something in there."

"Yeah, right," Tony Gritter sneered. "A secret tunnel. And I'm the president of the United States, too."

Holly shook her head. "I remember my dad telling me stories about a tunnel somewhere in Great Bear Heart. He said he didn't know where it was, but it's supposed to have been here for a long time."

Lyle Haywood laughed out loud, and Shane Mitchell rolled his eyes.

"Holly," Shane said, "we've been all over Great Bear Heart. We've never *ever* come across any tunnel."

As usual, we took a vote on whether or not we should investigate the door that Dylan had found. And, oddly enough, it was a tie vote. That's never happened in the Adventure Club before. Usually, most of our votes are unanimous. This time, myself, Holly and Dylan voted to investigate the door. Shane, Lyle and Tony voted against it.

"Now what do we do?" Tony asked, his voice filled with disgust. "How do we break the tie?"

"I don't care," Lyle Haywood said, glancing anxiously at his watch and then looking out the window. "All I know is that I'm wasting valuable fishing time. I could be hooking into the big one right now." He grabbed an imaginary fishing pole and pretended he was reeling in a fish.

Holly seized the opportunity. "The only big one you've ever hooked into," she said sharply, "was last summer when you messed up your cast and hooked yourself in the butt with a *Daredevil.*"

We all laughed. A *Daredevil* is a type of fishing lure called a 'spoon'. It's made out of metal, and it's a really good lure for northern pike. Lyle had accidentally hooked himself in his rear-end so badly that he needed to go to the hospital and have the treble hook removed. He even needed a couple stitches. None of us had actually witnessed the event, but we'd heard about it, and so had everyone else in Great Bear Heart.

"That wasn't my fault!" Lyle Haywood protested. "That wasn't—"

"—Okay, okay, enough," Shane Mitchell intervened. "Back to the door Dylan found. We had a tie vote, so we'll flip a coin." He stood up and dug into the pocket of his jeans. "Heads we go check it out, tails we forget the whole thing."

With a snap of his wrist and a flick of his thumb, he flipped a quarter into the air. It rose to the ceiling of the clubhouse, arched down, and thudded to the floor. We all watched it as it spun like a top on the rough wood. Finally, it came to a rest.

"Tails!" Lyle Haywood shouted triumphantly, shaking his fist in the air. "We forget about the stupid door! Yes! I'll see you guys later. I'm going fishin'." That said, Lyle opened up the trap door in the floor, slipped his skinny body through the square opening, shot Dylan a smirk, and vanished.

"Sorry about that," Shane said, turning to face Dylan "That's the breaks."

Dylan looked a bit dejected, but he didn't say anything. We talked about a few more things, and finally wrapped things up twenty minutes later. The meeting was adjourned, and we all went home.

All except Dylan Bunker. He was going to investigate

that door with or without the rest of the club. None of us were really interested in a hidden door at the old library.

But Dylan found something that changed our minds.

2

None of us saw Dylan Bunker until the next regular meeting of the Adventure Club. He was, of course, his usual fifteen minutes late. We passed the time listening to Lyle Haywood talk about how he had battled what he said was the biggest northern pike in Puckett Lake . . . only to have the monstrous beast break his line right at the boat. “It was as big as the pike we saw when we were exploring the lake in the submarine,” he said, spreading his arms wide. “In fact, that might have been the exact same fish!”

“The big one always gets away,” Tony Gritter snickered.

“Yeah, well, not next time,” Lyle replied curtly. “Next time, I’m gonna use my dad’s steel leaders. There’s no way I’m gonna lose that fish twice. He would’ve been a state record!"

Holly O'Mara glanced at me and rolled her eyes. I smiled. We were both accustomed to Lyle's fish tales.

Shane Mitchell remained silent, content to listen to Lyle and his fishing expeditions. When Dylan Bunker finally showed up, Shane called the meeting to order.

We went through the usual formalities, reviewing the minutes from the last meeting, talking about projects that we could do, things we could make, places we could go.

And through the entire meeting, Dylan Bunker didn't make a sound. He didn't speak, didn't offer any suggestions . . . which isn't like Dylan at all. He just sat quietly on his milk crate, watching and listening. Once, I heard him whistling softly to himself, like he hadn't a care in the world. I think he was smiling, but he was trying to hide it.

We weren't getting much done at this particular meeting. We talked about building some kind of glider or ultra-light plane that we could fly, but we've been talking about that for a year. Tony Gritter came up with an idea to sell pop and ice-cream down by the beach to make money, but we decided to put that topic on next week's agenda.

Shane stood up to call the meeting to a close.

"Anybody have anything to add?" he asked, glancing around the room.

Everyone looked around . . . *except* Dylan Bunker. Calmly, cooly, he pushed his hand into his jeans pocket and withdrew it. He opened up his hand, gazed into his palm and smiled, then clenched his fist. Without saying a word, he gently under-armed whatever he was holding in his hand.

A small object spun in the air, arced to the middle of the room, and clunked to the center of the floor. It landed with a heavy thud, and for a moment, I thought he'd tossed a rock.

It wasn't. It was a *coin.* A *large* coin at that, about the size of an old silver dollar—and, in fact, that's what it was!

The medallion rolled to a stop, dead center in the middle of our clubhouse. No one said a word. The only thing we could hear was the gentle rustling of leaves in the tree all around us.

Finally, Shane Mitchell bent over and picked up the coin. He flipped it over in his hands and let out a long whistle. Lines formed on his forehead as he raised his eyebrows in surprise.

"Where'd you find this?!?!?" he exclaimed excitedly.

Dylan Bunker wore a satisfied, cat-like grin that you couldn't have pried off with a crow bar.

"From the place you guys voted *not* to investigate," he said smartly, crossing his arms. He was pleased with himself, and it showed.

Tony Gritter rose to his feet and stood next to Shane. “Let me check that out,” he said, and in the next instant we were all huddled around Shane, each taking our turn holding and looking at the silver coin that Dylan had found.

It was quite old, and the date on one side read 1922. Many of the other letters were worn away, as were some of the features of the coin.

But it was definitely a silver dollar. It was tarnished and faded, and it was heavy.

“I’ll bet it’s pure silver!” Tony Gritter exclaimed. “It’s probably worth a fortune!”

“Actually, it *is* silver,” Dylan stated with a grin of satisfaction. “It’s called a ‘Peace Dollar’. They were made right after World War One. On one side is the liberty head, and on the other is an eagle, holding a laurel wreath. That was a symbol for peace after the war.”

We all turned and stared at Dylan Bunker. He seemed to know a lot about the coin . . . especially for someone who got a ‘C’ in history.

“I looked it up,” he continued, matter-of-factly. “In the library. There’s a book about old coins in there. It says that the one I found is probably worth around twenty dollars.”

He stood and walked toward our small circle, holding

out his hand. Shane dropped the coin into Dylan's palm.

"So," Dylan said, gently flipping the coin in the air and catching it again. *"Anyone wanna take a vote to investigate what's behind the door?"*

Our hands shot up into the air like rockets.

3

The Great Bear Heart Library is unique for a number of reasons, one of them being that the building used to be a railroad depot. In the 1800s, trains would bring vacationers from Detroit and Chicago to the quiet, peaceful town on Puckett Lake. In those days, there were two huge hotels, and Great Bear Heart was a lot bigger than it is today. The hotels burned down and were never re-built. Gradually, fewer and fewer tourists came. When the trains stopped coming, the railroad depot sat vacant for years, until it was split into two halves: one became the library, the other became the historical museum. The building was painted gray with white trim and it looks as good as new. You'll always know when the Great Bear Heart Library is open, because the librarian turns on a porch light during business hours.

But what else makes the library unique is that for one hour every day, it operates on the 'honor' system: Mrs. Norberg, the only librarian, takes a one-hour lunch-break, and leaves the door open. You can browse the books if you want, but you have to leave her a note to let her know which books you've borrowed. Even after the window-waxing incident a while back, the township still voted to leave the library open while Mrs. Norberg went home for lunch.

Try *that* in a big city library!

However, very few, if any, people visit the library during the lunch hour. Most people preferred to come to the library in the late afternoon or evening. We decided to wait until Mrs. Norberg went to lunch before we went to investigate the door Dylan had found.

We gathered at the market the following morning at eleven-thirty. I hardly slept a wink the night before, and I wasn't alone. We were all pretty geeked about finding out just what was behind that door.

And, more importantly, we were all pretty geeked about finding more old coins.

We were just *geeked,* period.

At noon, on the button, the old screen door opened, and Mrs. Norberg walked out. We waited until she was past the post office and on the way up the hill before we crossed the street.

I was so excited I could hardly contain myself.

4

Inside the library, Dylan hustled over to the room where he'd discovered the door. The Great Bear Heart Library is pretty small. It's split into a couple rooms, none of which are very large. It was amazing that a door could remain hidden there for all these years.

Yet, when Dylan showed us exactly where it was, it was easy to see just how the door had been missed by most people.

The bookshelf butted right up against the wall, and when the shelves were full of books, it was impossible to see the door. Dylan Bunker was right: the door was perfectly hidden.

"How did you get the door open?" Shane whispered to Dylan.

"Like this," Dylan replied. Carefully, he began taking all of the books from the top shelf. Holly O'Mara pitched in, and so did the rest of us. We stacked them in a pile on the floor.

"Be careful not to get them mixed up," Dylan said. "They all have to go back exactly where they came from."

In less than a minute the bookshelf was empty. Dylan reached forward, grabbed the side of the wood shelf, and slid it away from the wall. The old shelf creaked and groaned.

The door seemed to glare at us, as if daring us to open it. But the doorknob had been broken off.

Dylan was prepared for that. He reached into his pocket, pulled out his red-handled Swiss Army knife, and retracted a small, hooked can opener. Placing the curved part into the keyhole, he gave it a gentle twist, and then a tug.

The door popped open with a clunk and a chug. Dylan drew his knife back, and the door swung open slowly, as if it were opening by itself. The tired hinges squeaked and creaked, and cold, damp air drifted out. It smelled musky and old.

Aged wooden steps led down into darkness. The planks were dark gray and very weathered. The stairs descended down into gloom, and seemed to just disappear into black ink.

"They really don't go very far," Dylan explained, folding his knife and stuffing it back into the pocket of his jeans.

We all leaned forward, surrounding the door. It looked a little spooky, and, for a moment, I wondered if this was such a good idea after all.

Then I thought about the coin that Dylan had found, and I brushed away my apprehension.

"Lyle . . . did you bring the light?" Shane Mitchell asked.

Lyle Haywood reached into his knapsack, pulled out a heavy-duty flashlight, and clicked it on. The beam illuminated the dark steps, and we could see a dirt floor at the bottom.

Dylan Bunker was in his glory. He was proud of his discovery, proud that he alone had found something that we had been impressed by. He took charge.

"Let's go," he announced, taking the light from Lyle. "Follow me, gang."

5

At the bottom of the stairs, the air was chilly and damp. I wished I had worn a sweatshirt.

"I found the coin over here," Dylan said, sweeping the flashlight beam over the ground. "It was mostly buried in the dirt."

"I wonder what this used to be?" Holly O'Mara asked, looking around.

"I'll bet it was some old storage cellar a long time ago," Shane Mitchell offered.

Dylan shined the light along the wall. The walls and the ceiling were carefully constructed with old timbers. They were bent and stained with age, but they still appeared pretty solid.

"How far does this thing go?" I asked, pointing into the

darkness of the tunnel.

"Not far," Dylan replied. "Right there, as a matter of fact." He shined his light up, illuminating a brick wall. The stones were reddish-brown colored, and looked wet and grimy.

"Shine it on the ground again," Tony Gritter said. "I wanna find one of those silver dollars."

Dylan shined the light at our feet and we all dropped to our knees, searching. The flashlight did a pretty good job of brightening up the small tunnel, and each of us dug our hands into the dirt, sifting it through our fingers. The dirt was cold, and it made my hands feel greasy. Once, I felt a lump between my fingers, and I almost shouted with joy. I thought I'd found a silver dollar. It turned out to be a rock.

We sifted and searched for a long time. As the minutes ticked by, it became apparent that there probably weren't any more coins. None of us had any luck, and we became frustrated.

"I'll bet you didn't even find that down coin here," Tony Gritter chided Dylan. "I'll bet you swiped that old coin from your dad's collection."

Dylan was infuriated. "Did not!" he defended. "I found it right here!" His cheeks reddened, and his eyes grew dark. "If you guys would've voted to come and check out the door, you'd have seen for yourself!"

"Chill out, Dylan," Lyle Haywood urged, his voice easy and calm. "We believe you. It's just that you probably found the *only* coin that was here. No big deal. It's still kind of a cool place. I'm glad we came."

Finally, Shane placed his arm under the beam of the flashlight and looked at his watch.

"Twelve forty-five," he reported. "We gotta go. Mrs. Norberg will be back soon."

I was kind of disappointed. I wished we would have found some silver coins. That would've really been cool.

I stood up and began walking toward the steps. Lyle was next to me, and Tony was right behind me.

"Wait," Holly O'Mara's voice rang out softly from the darkness. "Wait just a second."

The three of us stopped. Dylan Bunker shined the light down the tunnel. Holly was there, and her back was to us. She was looking at the brick wall.

"Something is strange here," she said curiously. "It's almost like . . . like I can feel a draft. There's air coming in from someplace."

Shane Mitchell walked toward her, and his form suddenly appeared in the beam of the flashlight. Holly and he stood next to each other, facing the wall. Shane raised his hand and slowly waved it in front of the bricks.

"She's right!" he said excitedly, turning toward us. "There's a draft coming in from somewhere! Dylan . . . bring that light over here!"

Dylan walked toward Shane. Tony, Lyle, and I followed, our interest aroused.

Shane took the light from Dylan and he pointed the beam up at the top of the brick wall. It seemed to be pretty solid, and there weren't any holes that we could see.

The beam traveled to the ground, but, once again, there didn't appear to be anyplace where air could get through.

"No, not there," Holly said. "Here. Shine it up here."

Shane pointed the beam back up at the brick wall.

"The air seems to be coming from along these cracks," she said, running her finger in the crease between two bricks. "It's almost like this is a—"

She stopped speaking, and her hand stopped. She gently nudged and poked at one of the bricks. "I can feel air right here," she said.

"Nope," snickered Tony Gritter. "That was just me. I had baked beans for lunch."

Dylan Bunker giggled and Lyle Haywood snorted. I chuckled a bit.

Holly ignored Tony's remark. She placed her entire hand on the brick, and pushed.

The cement block fell away, exposing a gaping, black

hole exactly three inches high by six inches wide. Stale air poured out like water, like an enormous balloon with a leak.

Wow! It was a *false wall!* There was a room—or something—on the other side!

6

"Whoah!" Lyle Haywood whispered. "It's a fake wall!"

"I wonder how far it goes?" I asked. We were all leaning forward now, trying to look through rectangular, dark hole in the brick wall.

Shane Mitchell raised the light up and poked the beam through the small opening. He pushed another brick with his free hand, and the heavy block disappeared, tumbling to the ground with a thud on the other side of the wall. Shane's arm passed through the light, and he glanced at his watch.

"Smokes!" he piped. "It's twelve fifty-five! We've only got five minutes to get out of here and get the books back on the shelf!"

Further investigation of the mysterious brick wall

would have to wait. Immediately, we all turned and scrambled back toward the steps. Our feet thundered on the old boards as we flew up the stairs and out the door.

"Quick!" Tony Gritter barked. "Get that shelf against the door!"

Holly and I pushed the bookshelf back into place while Shane, Tony, Lyle, and Dylan began picking up books. We had barely got the rack in place when they started hastily filing the volumes back onto the shelf.

"Careful!" I cautioned. "Make sure they get back on the shelf in order!"

Shane glanced at his watch —just as Dylan looked out the window.

"She's coming!" he hissed.

He was right! I shot a quick glimpse out the window, and saw Mrs. Norberg walking by the post office, on her way back from lunch. She'd be here in less than a minute!

"We can do it!" Holly O'Mara insisted. "Keep going!"

Books were flying back onto the shelf. The entire series of *Hardy Boys* books (minus number 28, of course) flashed in front of me, quickly returning to the shelf in numerical order. Just as the last books were being placed on the bottom shelf, we heard the door of the library creak open.

Whew! Just in time.

Mrs Norberg came in and saw us standing in the room adjacent to her small office. She was carrying a small pile of papers, a green folder, and the day's mail.

"Well, it looks like we've been visited by some bookworms," she said, smiling. Mrs. Norberg is a nice lady, and pretty much gets along with everyone. All of us like her a lot.

We just didn't want her to know that we'd been taking apart the library to go through a door that we probably weren't supposed to in the first place.

"Oh, we were just taking a look," Lyle Haywood said, grinning innocently.

"Find anything interesting?" Mrs. Norberg asked. She set the papers, folder, and mail onto her desk. She smiled, looking at each of us, and I couldn't help but wonder if she knew.

"Well, yes," Holly O'Mara replied. "Yes, we did."

"Good, that's good," Mrs. Norberg responded.

And that was pretty much the extent of the conversation. We said good-bye to Mrs. Norberg, and told her that we'd all be back soon. We all figured that we'd made a clean break—but she spoke up just as Dylan was about to close the library door behind him.

"Mr. Bunker." Mrs. Norberg's voice was cold and serious. "I'd like to see you for a moment, if I could."

We all froze. Dylan had a terrified expression on his face, and his eyes were huge. He looked like a deer caught in the headlights of an oncoming car.

"M . . .m . . . me?" he stammered, glancing around at each one of us.

"Yes, *you,"* Mrs. Norberg replied curtly.

And she wasn't smiling.

7

Shane, Tony, Lyle, Holly, and I ran around the building to the other side. A window was open, and we could peer inside to see what was happening.

"Mr. Bunker," Mrs. Norberg began, "a piece if library property has been missing for some time. I think perhaps, you are aware of this."

Dylan Bunker just about fell out of his chair.

"But . . . but . . . ." he sputtered. "I didn't . . . I mean, I, uh . . . ."

Mrs. Norberg smiled, her face beaming. "I just wanted to let you know that it's been found." She reached into her desk and pulled out the missing copy of *The Hardy Boys #28: The Sign of the Crooked Arrow.* "I discovered it in the encyclopedia section, behind the books on the floor," she explained. She handed the book to Dylan, and he took it with trembling hands. Relief welled up inside of him. He was certain that he'd been caught red-handed with the coin that he'd found behind the hidden door.

"Th . . . thank you," he said, glancing down at the book, and then at Mrs. Norberg.

"You're welcome," she answered, still smiling.

Dylan stood up and left without saying anything more. We sneaked around the side of the library, crossed the street, and met up with him at the market.

"Man, was I freaked out!" he said, waving the book with one hand and shaking his head. "I thought I was busted for sure!" He explained about the missing *Hardy Boys* book, and we all drew a collective sigh of relief.

But our excitement was at a boiling point. We had just discovered that the brick wall was phony, and there was something behind it.

Why had someone built a false wall?

We filed into the Great Bear Heart Market. I bought an ice-cream bar and a pack of gum. Holly O'Mara bought a bottle of apple juice, and everyone else bought ice-cream cones. We left, and walked across the street to the park. The wind hissed gently through the tall trees, and children played at the small park beach under the watchful eyes of their parents. A golden retriever was chasing a frisbee that someone had thrown, and a teenage girl, laughing and screaming, was being tossed off the dock by several of her friends. Black-capped chickadees flirted in the trees above.

The six of us sat down at a picnic table, and began discussing what might be behind the wall.

"Maybe bank robbers stashed their loot down there," Lyle Haywood mused.

"It might be a gold mine!" Dylan Bunker exclaimed hopefully, slurping on an ice-cream cone. He had creamy vanilla goo all around his mouth.

"There's never been any gold mines in Great Bear Heart," Holly O'Mara replied, rolling her eyes.

"I'll bet there are dead bodies back there," Tony Gritter offered with a sly smile. He, too, was eating an ice-cream cone, and he popped the last bit of it into his mouth after he spoke.

"Get outta here," Shane Mitchell said, shaking his head. "You guys are just dreaming. There's probably nothing there but dirt."

But somebody had spent a lot of time constructing that brick wall. What could possibly be behind it, and why?

Perhaps the worst part about it was that now we had to wait until tomorrow at noon—when Mrs. Norberg went to lunch—to go back and investigate. I didn't think I was going to be able to wait that long. A whole day? I thought

I was going to go crazy. The next day would never be able to come fast enough.

Well, it did . . . and it wouldn't be long before I was wishing the exact opposite. Soon, I'd be wishing that we never even set foot in that tunnel.

8

The next day, we held an early morning meeting at the clubhouse. Dylan Bunker was his usual fifteen minutes late, but so was Holly O'Mara. She'd spent the morning helping her mom around the house.

We all agreed to bring a few things. First off, we all brought flashlights. That was mandatory. Holly O'Mara brought a box of matches and a candle, and Shane Mitchell brought his boy scout first-aid kit. Lyle Haywood brought his knapsack, complete with a compass and a few other odds and ends. Dylan Bunker brought his Swiss Army knife, and Tony Gritter brought a ball of twine. We would tie one end of the twine to the door and let it out as we went into the tunnel. That way we wouldn't get lost, in case we found side tunnels or passageways.

But I was sure we'd be fine. I was certain that the tunnel couldn't go very far. Maybe a few dozen feet at the most. The more I thought about it, the more I thought that we might be wasting our time and getting all worked up over nothing.

The day was hazy, hot and humid, and the sky was a steely-gray. There was no wind. The air was thick and heavy, and we were all perspiring by the time noon rolled around. Once again, we hung out at the Great Bear Heart Market, waiting for Mrs. Norberg to leave for lunch.

Bingo. At noon, right on the money, the library door opened up. Mrs. Norberg left, carrying a large purse in one hand, and an armload of papers in the other. We waited until she was on her way up the hill.

"Let's go," Shane said, and we strode calmly across the street, taking our time—just in case anyone was watching. I didn't know why we were being so secretive about it. It's not like we were really doing anything wrong. I guess maybe it was because we'd found something, and we just didn't want anyone to know about it yet.

Getting back into the tunnel was easy. In no time at all we had removed the books, backed the shelf away from the wall, and opened the door. Seconds later we were in the dark cavern, standing at the brick wall.

"Let's be careful," I advised. "Instead of pushing those

bricks in, let's pull them out and stack them up. It will be easier to put them back."

Everyone agreed that this would be a good idea, and we got to work. With the six of us pulling out the bricks and piling them up, we had the entire wall down in only a few minutes.

Before us was a dark tunnel. With the six flashlights,

we illuminated the cavern pretty well. The walls of the tunnel were lined with bricks. After a dozen feet or so the brickwork ended, exposing rough, jagged stone. Beneath our feet was solid rock, covered with a fine layer of dirt and dust. Whatever this tunnel was, it wasn't made by any man. The bricks had only been constructed to give the small a room-like quality. This was a tunnel that had probably been here for thousands of years.

My heart was racing. This was just *too* cool.

"Come on," Tony Gritter urged, taking a step forward. "We've only got fifty minutes." He'd already tied one end of the ball of twine to the door at the top of the steps, and he began letting it out as he walked down the tunnel.

"I wonder where this thing goes?" Dylan Bunker asked.

"Probably to Timbuktu," Tony snickered. "All tunnels lead to Timbuktu."

Our voices sounded strange in the tunnel. They echoed a little, but the sound didn't seem to carry very far. I felt like I had to talk louder just so the rest of the group would hear me, even though we were all pretty close together.

As we walked, my eyes kept scanning the ground. I think everyone else was searching, too. We were all hoping we'd find a silver dollar like the one Dylan Bunker had found.

We'd only walked about a hundred feet when the tunnel suddenly split. We stopped. A smaller, thinner passageway went off to the right. Shane Mitchell swept his flashlight back and forth between the two tunnels. Both looked the same, except the tunnel that veered off to the right was much smaller. Any one of us would have to duck to keep our heads from hitting the roof of the tunnel.

"Okay," Shane said. "Lyle and I will see where this one goes. Everyone else wait right here. We'll take the ball of twine with us, so we can follow it back."

I didn't like the idea of splitting up, but I guessed it would be okay as along at Shane and Lyle had the ball of twine.

They stepped into the small tunnel and vanished into the darkness. We could hear their voices and footsteps for a few seconds, but even those sounds disappeared quickly. The four of us—Dylan, Holly, Tony, and myself—waited.

"I wonder how many other people know about this?" Holly asked. "And has this tunnel been blocked off? Those bricks look like they hadn't been touched in years."

I turned off my flashlight to save the batteries. If we were just standing around, there was no need to use my light. Holly turned hers off as well, but Dylan and Tony left theirs on.

"Let me see that silver dollar again, Dylan," I said.

Dylan Bunker stuffed his hand into his pocket and brought out a wrinkled zip-lock bag. He unraveled it and opened it up, and the coin fell into his palm. He handed it to me, and I held it under Tony's flashlight beam.

"Man, I sure would like to get my hands on a few of those," Tony yearned, peering down at the dollar in my hand.

I flipped the coin over in my hands, thinking the exact same thing as Tony. It sure would be cool to find a whole chest full of silver dollars. Heck, it would be cool just to find *one* silver dollar.

Just as I handed the coin back to Dylan, we heard a panic-stricken shriek echoing from the small tunnel to the right. The sound shocked all of us and we spun.

It was Shane and Lyle! They sounded far off, and we couldn't tell what they were saying, but man—they were screaming their heads off!

9

I fumbled with my flashlight. Dylan had already brought his up and was pointing it down the dark cavern where Shane and Lyle had gone. The only thing we could see was the twine as it disappeared around a dark, jagged corner.

I flicked my light on and shined it down the tunnel, but it didn't help much. Shane and Lyle were still screaming, but their voices were far away and unintelligible. I couldn't make out what they were saying. One thing was for sure: they were frantic.

"We've got to help them!" Holly cried, and the four of us ducked our heads low and bolted into the small tunnel.

We didn't get far.

"What was that?!?!" Dylan Bunker suddenly shrieked. He'd seen something, and he cowered down low, covering

his head with his arm. A movement in the tunnel ahead caught my attention, and I, too, ducked as something went whizzing by my head.

"BATS!" Tony Gritter suddenly howled.

"Hit the deck!" I shouted, and the four of us immediately dropped to the ground, covering our heads with our hands. Flashlight beams went flying as we crashed to the cavern floor.

The bats poured out of the tunnel like flying demons. Not ten, not twenty or thirty—but hundreds of them. *Thousands* of them. All we could hear was the sound of their wings whirring past, and their tiny, high-pitched squeals as they flew overhead. It was like a squeaky freight train was rolling right over top of us!

I kept my hands over my head and my face to the ground. Some people claim that bats get tangled up in your hair, but that's just an old wives' tale.

Still, I wasn't taking any chances. Besides . . . I read somewhere that bats can carry rabies. A friend from school was bitten by a bat once, and he said he had to go to the hospital and have shots so he wouldn't get sick.

That's nothing I wanted to mess with, that's for sure.

The bats continued streaking by for what seemed like hours. Actually, it was less than a minute, but it sure seemed like a lot longer. I could hear them all around, and some of them whizzed only inches from my ear! The fleeing swarm filled the entire tunnel.

Finally, the drone of flapping wings dwindled to only a few sporadic bats, and I cautiously pulled my hands from my head and looked up. A single bat spun from around the corner and flew past, followed by another. Then the bats were gone.

I hoped.

"All clear, I think," I said, poking my head up a bit more. I scrambled to my knees, and then to my feet, brushing myself off. Holly O'Mara did the same, followed by Tony Gritter. Dylan remained crouched low to the ground, still unsure if it was safe to get up. He wasn't taking any chances.

A noise came from the tunnel, giving us all a start. We were ready to hit the ground again, in case more bats came through.

A flashlight beam appeared, and we heard giggling. Soon, the shapes of Shane Mitchell and Lyle Haywood emerged, walking toward us. Lyle was winding up the twine back around the ball as he drew closer.

"Did you see those bats?!?!?" Shane exclaimed.

"How could we miss them?" I gasped. "They were everywhere!"

"They sure surprised *us,"* Lyle Haywood said.

"You aren't the only ones," Holly O'Mara reiterated.

"Yeah, that sure was freaky," Dylan Bunker chimed in, finally getting to his feet. "There must've been a bajillion of them!"

"I've told you a gazillion times not to exaggerate," Tony Gritter sneered. Dylan ignored the jibe.

"The tunnel dead ends after a few hundred feet," Lyle explained. "There's a big cavern with a high ceiling. That's where the bats came from. They were all hanging from the top of the cave. Man . . . it sure did stink in there! Shane threw a rock to see what the bats would do."

Holly O'Mara rolled her eyes.

"Well, we know one thing," Shane Mitchell said. "There's another way out of here, that's for sure. Those bats got in here somehow, and it wasn't through the brick wall. That means this tunnel definitely goes *somewhere.*"

And so, we were off. Those bats had to get out of the tunnel somehow, like Shane said. There was another entrance, another way to get into the tunnel— and we were going to find it.

Of course, we were still quite interested in finding a stash of coins, but that seemed more and more unlikely as time went on.

We walked deeper into the tunnel. All of us had our flashlights on, and the inside of the narrow cavern was lit up like daylight.

After about five minutes of walking, the ball of twine ran out. We all voted in favor of continuing on, just as long as we didn't venture off into any side tunnels, should we happen upon any more. Without the twine to follow back, it would be too easy to get lost.

The deeper we traveled, the narrower the tunnel became. Soon, we all had to stoop to walk, and the walls had closed in so much that we had to walk single-file.

Shane was in the lead. After a few more minutes of very difficult walking and crouching, he stopped, forcing us all to do the same.

"This thing goes on forever," he moaned. "We've got to be half way across the county by now."

"I just wonder where it comes out at," Lyle Haywood questioned. "I mean . . . we haven't come across those bats. They had to go somewhere."

"Wait a minute!" Holly O'Mara suddenly gasped from behind me. Her voice was tense, serious. "The bats went somewhere . . . but what if they come back? *They have to come back through this tunnel!"*

We all knew what she was getting at. Bats are nocturnal, meaning they sleep during the day and hunt for food at night. We had disturbed them during their sleep, so it was only reasonable to think that they'd be returning soon to go back to their cave.

And where we were, the tunnel was so narrow that if the bats came back through, they'd be swarming all around us!

Gulp!

The thought of a million of the little buggers fluttering past, bumping into me, screeching and squealing, didn't make me feel very comfortable.

Shane Mitchell raised his arm and shined a light on his watch. "It's time to go, anyway," he said. "We've got to head back. So much for finding any treasure today."

Fine with me. Now that Holly had brought up the fact that the bats might be coming back, I was more than happy to high-tail it out of there.

We all did an about-face and began walking. Our sneakers were silent on the powdery dirt beneath our feet. Soon, the tunnel widened, and we had more room to walk. It sure was a lot easier going when we didn't have to stoop over and hike at the same time.

Dylan spotted the twine on the ground and he picked it up, winding it around his arm as he walked.

"Geez you guys," he said dejectedly. "I'm sorry we didn't find any more coins. I really thought we would." He hung his head as he walked. He really felt bad about not finding any more silver dollars.

"No big deal," I said. "This has been pretty cool. I bet no one else in Great Bear Heart knows about this place. I'm glad you found it. It's kind of like our very own secret tunnel."

"Yeah," Holly chimed in, trying to cheer up Dylan. "This was kind of fun." She tossed a nervous glance over her shoulder, as we all had been doing, wary of any bats that might appear. None of us wanted to be in the cavern when those bats returned.

Soon, we passed the tunnel where Shane and Lyle had spooked the bats, and we all let out a collective sigh of relief. If the bats returned to their cave, we'd be safe. We wouldn't be in their path.

But there was a major problem in our thinking. A *major* one . . . and we were about to get the shock of our lives.

10

We arrived at the pile of bricks that made up the dismantled wall. As soon as we saw the light from the open door at the top of the stairs, Tony Gritter grabbed my arm.

"Wait," he said, in a voice just above a whisper. *"Listen!"*

We all stopped, our ears perked and attentive.

"I hear it!" Holly O'Mara said. "But . . . what is it?"

There was a noise all right, and it sounded like it was coming from the library.

"Do you think that someone's in the library?" I asked quietly.

Shane shook his head. "That doesn't sound like people," he said. "That sounds like—that sounds like . . . *bats!"*

Oh no! Was it possible?

Holly O'Mara drew in a sudden, deep breath, and her hands covered her mouth.

"Guys," Tony Gritter said seriously. "We are in deep doo-doo. *Deep* doo-doo. We are in doo-doo up to our necks."

It was true. As we approached the stairs that led back up to the library, our worst fears were confirmed.

The bats had traveled through the tunnel, all right—*but they had followed it back to the library!* We had left the door open, and they had probably followed an air current flowing through the tunnel.

Which meant—

I couldn't bear the thought.

The bats were in the library!

Shane was first up the steps, but he halted abruptly before he reached the open door. He leaned forward, craning his neck and looking up. We followed behind him, and stopped when he stopped.

"What?" asked Dylan Bunker from behind me. "What is it?" He was a couple of steps lower, and we were blocking his view. He couldn't see what was going on.

"Holy grass snakes!" Shane exclaimed, his head tilted back. He was still standing on the steps, looking up into the library. "We've really done it this time! Oh, man! There are bats *everywhere!"*

I poked my head around Tony Gritter to get a look over Shane's shoulder. I couldn't see much, but what I saw sent a wave of shivers down my spine.

It was a *calamity!* From where I stood, I could look up through the open door and see bats everywhere! They were darting through the air, hanging from the ceiling, from the bookshelves . . . from *everything!* The room was filled with high-pitched squeals and the hiss of fluttering wings.

Man, oh, man . . . we'd really screwed things up. The bats were going to make a terrible mess!

It was at this point that I knew I'd be grounded for life. I'd be grounded for life, but, with any hope, I'd get ungrounded for good behavior—in about forty years.

The six of us stood on the stairs, wondering what to do. How do you get thousands of bats out of a small area like the library?

All of a sudden, there was a loud *whooshing* sound, the sound of . . . *the library door opening!*

"Oh no!" Shane Mitchell exclaimed, glancing at his watch. "Mrs. Norberg is due back from lunch *right now!"*

And then we heard it. A loud scream came from outside.

We all knew what it meant. Things were about to go from bad . . . *to worse.*

11

The fluttering of wings in the library above us became a dull roar as more and more bats took flight. Shane bounded up the steps, keeping his head low. He stepped up into the library, poked his head through the open door, and peered around the corner.

Mrs. Norberg began shrieking at the very top of her lungs.

"Eeeeek! Eeeeeek!" she screeched as she ran from the library. I really felt bad for her. She'd dropped her purse and armload of papers, and the documents began blowing across the parking lot.

Shane looked down at us from the top of the stairs. "Mrs. Norberg left the door open!" he blurted. "The bats are flying out through the front door! Now's our chance!

We can get out of here!" Shane stepped through the open door and into the library.

Tony Gritter, Holly O'Mara, Lyle Haywood, Dylan Bunker and I bounded up the steps and into the room, keeping our heads low. Above us, a cloud of bats swarmed and circled. I bobbed and weaved whenever one came close to my head.

Tony pulled the door closed behind us, and Dylan pushed the shelf back up against the wall.

"Let's get these books back on the shelf!" Shane hissed. *"If we hurry, we can put everything back into place and sneak through the back door!"*

The Great Bear Heart Library has a rear exit—a fire exit—that nobody uses. The door faces the roadside park on Puckett Lake. With any luck, we'd be able to get out the back door and high-tail it down to the lake without anyone being the wiser.

I shot a quick glance outside.

On the other side of the street, Mrs. Norberg stood on the sidewalk. A small crowd of people had gathered, some pointing at the library, others staring up into the sky as the bats continued to pour out through the front door.

In the library, there were still hundreds of bats frantically buzzing overhead, but their numbers were dwindling as they found the open door. Soon, they'd be gone.

"Come on, come on!" Shane Mitchell coaxed. We double-timed our efforts, and books literally flew back to the shelves.

Finally, when the last of the books had been replaced, Lyle Haywood charged toward the fire exit. He pushed the door open and leapt outside, and the rest of us almost piled on top of him as we tumbled through. Dylan Bunker fell into Holly O'Mara, who fell into me. I collapsed to the ground, followed by Holly, and then Dylan, who landed on top of us.

"Get . . . off . . . me!" I heaved, struggling to get back up. Dylan Bunker got to his feet, then Holly, then me. With Shane, Tony, and Lyle ahead of the three of us, we dashed over the old railroad track and dashed down the hill into the park. Thankfully, there were only a few people seated at the picnic tables, and no one seemed to pay any attention to the group of six kids that wandered through at a brisk walk.

"That was close," I said, glancing back toward the library.

"You're not kidding!" Dylan Bunker agreed, breathing a sigh relief.

"Poor Mrs. Norberg," Holly O'Mara grieved, shaking her head. "I'm sure those bats nearly scared her to death." We all felt terrible about scaring Mrs. Norberg like that.

We walked through the park and up a side trail, back over the railroad tracks, and crossed the highway to the hardware store.

Down the street, the scene was chaotic. Mrs. Norberg was still standing on the sidewalk, a safe distance from the library. A crowd had gathered, and they were all looking at the library in wonder. Some of the people were leaning back, their heads tilted upward, scanning the skies.

"Come on," Tony Gritter said, walking ahead. He turned, flashing us a mischievous grin. "Let's go see what all of the commotion is about."

By the time we passed the market, a fire engine had arrived, sirens blaring and lights flashing, followed by a police car. Apparently, bats in the library was big news in the tiny town of Great Bear Heart.

Norm Beeblemeyer, the reporter from the *Great Bear Heart Times* was already there, taking pictures and asking all kinds of questions. We were careful not to get too close, and equally careful to make sure that none of us smiled. We didn't want to let on that we knew anything.

The town gossip, Lucy Marbles, was there, wearing a blue bathrobe and fuzzy white slippers. Her hair was in curlers, and she carried a dish towel. She was giving everyone her account of what had happened. "Bats," she was saying, spreading her arms wide. "The size of seagulls. Teeth like a mountain lion." As she said this, she opened her mouth, exposing her own teeth, as if that would appear more threatening. "They were everywhere," she claimed, throwing her arms into the air. "Came right outta the library and attacked poor Mrs. Norberg! Why, she was lucky to escape with her life!"

This caused Tony Gritter to let out a choking laugh, but he quickly caught himself. Norm Beeblemeyer heard Tony's chuckle and shot us a nasty look, then continued jotting something down on a pad of yellow paper. Mrs. Marbles chatted away, and by the way she told the story, you would've thought she'd witnessed the whole thing. Actually, she hadn't seen the bats at all. From her house, she'd spotted the ruckus from her kitchen window, and, true to her nature, she just *had* to know what was going on. From the tiny bits of information that she was able to gobble up from the other people around, she was able to concoct her own wild story. Dozens of people stood by, listening to her amazing tale.

12

The headline in the *Great Bear Heart Times* that week was hilarious. *MYSTERY BATS INVADE LIBRARY,* read the big block letters. Right beneath was a photo of Lucy Marbles, arms spread, her mouth open, like she was showing her fangs. She looked ridiculous. The article hardly even mentioned poor Mrs. Norberg, who we all felt kind of sorry for. She'd been pretty frightened by the whole ordeal, but she hadn't been hurt. No one in Great Bear Heart seemed to know where the bats had came from, or where they went.

But Mr. Farnell, who runs the hardware store, had a pretty good idea.

I was walking home from the market when I saw Mr. Farnell. He was sitting in a lawn chair in front of his store, reading the paper, smiling and shaking his head. I couldn't resist.

"Watch out for those huge bats," I grinned, mocking Mrs. Marbles by making a flying gesture with my arms.

Mr. Farnell lowered his paper, smiled back. He leaned back in his chair and looked up into the sky. Then, frowning, he said, "you know, as a boy, I recall there was a big problem with bats. This was long before the library, though. It was back when the building was still a train depot."

"No kidding?" I asked, my interest piqued.

"Yep," he replied, nodding toward the library. "See, there's a tunnel that goes all the way from where the library is—" he raised his arm and pointed with his thumb, and continued, "—all the way out to Devil's Ridge."

So that was where the tunnel came out! I've never been to Devil's Ridge, but I knew it wasn't too far from town. My eyes lit up, and I listened intently to Mr. Farnell.

"The bats used to come swarming through the old storage cellar. Even with the door closed, the bats could smoosh their bodies as thin as a piece of cardboard and shimmy right on through the crack in the door." Mr. Farnell placed his thumb almost to his forefinger, showing me how small of a crack the bats could get through. "They finally had to brick up the tunnel to keep'em from comin' into the building," he explained.

But here was the real interesting part:

Mr. Farnell went on to say that, not long before the brick wall had been built, there had been a bank robbery in Detroit. The crooks hopped a train and headed north, and the police chased them . . . but they lost the trail here in Great Bear Heart. Two weeks later, the police caught up with them. They were hiding out in the tunnel beneath the train depot! The cops chased them all the way up to a house on the hill behind the post office. The three robbers died in a shoot-out with police, but the stolen money was never found.

"Do you remember what was stolen?" I asked Mr. Farnell. "Like, was it hundred dollar bills, or something?"

Mr. Farnell leaned back, nodding. "Yes," he replied. "Yes I do remember. It was coins. *Silver dollars, to be exact. A whole chest of silver dollars. The cops never found the money.*"

I thought my jaw was going to hit the floor.

13

And so the mystery of the tunnel behind the hidden door was solved. It all made sense now. The tunnel had always been there—long before the depot. The old train station had been built around it. The brick wall had been erected, years ago, to keep the bats from flying into the old railroad depot.

But now that the wall was down, I'm sure the bats would find a way to slip through the door again, only not so many of them, and not at the same time. Mrs. Norberg would find out what the problem was, and the township would put the bricks back up—if the wall hadn't already been re-erected. The only mystery for anyone to solve would be how the bricks got down in the first place.

But now we were faced with another mystery: just

where had the chest of silver dollars gone?

At the next regular meeting of the Adventure Club, I told everyone what Mr. Farnell had explained to me.

"See?!?!" Dylan Bunker exclaimed proudly. He drilled his chest with his thumb. "I *knew* there were more silver dollars! I *knew* it! Let's go search that house!"

"Chill, Dylan," Tony Gritter said. "There is no way those dollars will be there. That's the second place the police would have looked. The first place would have been the tunnel, and we already know there's no chest full of money there."

Mr. Farnell had said that he thought the tunnel came out somewhere near Devil's Ridge. We all knew where that was. Devil's Ridge was on the other side of town, quite a ways away from any houses or buildings. None of us had actually been to the ridge before. We'd never heard of any entrance to any cave, but, then again, we'd never asked anyone about it.

And so, we voted to investigate. We knew it was a long shot, but we figured that maybe, somehow, the crooks had possibly stashed the loot in the tunnel near Devil's Ridge. It was decided that we would all meet at the clubhouse on Saturday morning, hike over to the ridge, and see if we could find where the tunnel came out.

We didn't find any silver dollars—that would come

later.

What we did find, however, was an old, old cemetery. And what followed was one of the wildest, craziest—and *strangest*—adventures of the summer.

Ghost in the Graveyard

1

I don't believe in ghosts, and I'm not afraid of them.

Period. They don't exist.

However, I'm not sure how to explain what happened in the old cemetery we found not far from Devil's Ridge.

Maybe ghosts *do* exist, after all.

The whole thing got started because the club had voted to try and find a chest of stolen silver dollars that had been missing since a bank robbery in Detroit many years ago. No one knew exactly where the money was, but we decided we'd hunt around a bit and see what we could find.

We thought a good place to start would be the other end of a little-known underground tunnel that stretched from what is now the Great Bear Heart Library, all the way out to Devil's Ridge. I guess we really didn't expect to find any money way out there, but it was as good of a place as any to start.

We didn't find any silver coins, but you might say we found a bit more than what we bargained for.

If you ask anyone in Great Bear Heart just where Devil's Ridge is located, they're bound to give you a funny look, and say something like 'gee, I've never heard of that place before', or 'hmmm, I don't think there *is* a 'Devil's Ridge' in Great Bear Heart.

Don't you believe it. It's there, all right. It's just that no one likes to talk about it, and, as far as we can tell, no one goes there anymore.

We were about to find out why.

As usual, the six of us—Shane Mitchell, Holly O'Mara, Tony Gritter, Lyle Haywood, Dylan Bunker, and myself—met at our clubhouse high in the maple tree on the other side of McArdle's farm. The morning was gray and overcast, and it had rained hard overnight. The downpour had stopped about an hour ago, leaving the leaves on the trees all shiny and wet. There's a leak in the roof of our clubhouse at the southwest corner, and when we arrived in the morning, the blue coffee can that we use to catch the drips was overflowing. It must have rained most of the night.

We waited for Dylan Bunker to arrive, and, this

morning, no one gave him any grief for being fifteen minutes late. I don't think anyone was in a big hurry to go traipsing through the wet forest.

Shane called the meeting to order.

"Okay," he said. "Since we're headed out to Devil's Ridge, I motion that we move any and all business to the next meeting."

"Seconded," Holly O'Mara agreed.

"I motion we wait till everything dries up," Tony Gritter suggested. No one raised their hand or spoke. Tony was out-voted.

"First motion passed," Shane replied. "We hike to Devil's Ridge. Let's go."

This was going to be one of our easier adventures. We didn't have to build anything, pack anything, spend any money for anything. We were just going to hike back to the Ridge and see if we could find the tunnel. Then, we would see if we could find the missing chest of silver dollars.

We rode our bikes along what is called the Great Bear Heart Mail Route Road, until we reached the place where the power lines cross. There's a swath of trees cut through the forest to make room for the electrical poles. A faint, two-track trail runs beneath the power lines. In the summer, the passage is used infrequently, but in the winter, it becomes a pretty busy snowmobile trail.

We turned right onto the two-track, and rode our bikes along the path. Rain-drenched brush and ferns licked at our legs, and, pretty soon, most of us were soaked from our knees down to our shoes.

After about a quarter of a mile, we stopped. Lyle was in front; he knew where we needed to go.

"Over there," he said, pointing through the woods. There was no trail, and we'd have to leave our bikes at the two-track and hike the rest of the way. Most of us knew the general area around the ridge, but Lyle has been around there the most. He says there's good hunting in the thick swamps near Devil's Ridge.

We knew we were in for a hike. Not a real long one, mind you . . . but it was bound be a wet one. With all of the trees and branches still dripping wet from the overnight rain, we knew we were going to get soaked to the bone—even worse than we already were.

What we didn't know was that, at that very moment, we were being followed.

2

"There it is," Lyle said, stopping and raising his arm. We all stopped and looked where he was pointing.

On the other side of a small valley was Devil's Ridge. There's a sharp ledge that juts out at the top of a small, steep, hill. Actually, it almost looks like a tiny mountain. The rocks are dark gray, and today they blended in almost perfectly with the ashen sky overhead. Trees in the valley, and along the hill, swayed in the wind. It was actually kind of eerie looking.

From where we stood, a hill slopes down through a thick stand of evergreens. There's a weathered, over-grown trail that winds through the trees right to the foot of Devil's Ridge. Lyle began walking down the thin path.

"Wait a minute," Dylan Bunker paused. "If we go that

way, we'll get soaked even worse than we already are. Those branches are all wet, and there's no way we'll get through without hitting them."

"That's okay," Tony Gritter scoffed. "I talked to your mommy this morning, and she says that it's okay if you get wet."

Dylan shot Tony a nasty glance.

"Dylan's right," Holly O'Mara agreed. "It would be just as easy to go around the trees and go through that field over there." She pointed past the evergreens to an expanse of tall, wisping grass. The blades were shiny and bowed, heavy with water.

"Fine with me," Lyle shrugged nonchalantly, changing the direction of his lead. "Six of one, half-dozen of the other." He headed toward the field of tall grass, and we followed.

"Where do you think the tunnel comes out?" I wondered aloud.

"My guess," Shane Mitchell answered, stepping over a log. He glanced upward and pointed as we continued walking. "My guess is that it's somewhere right up near the ridge. Hidden up under the ledge somewhere."

I glanced up again at the stone cliff. It sure looked weird for some reason. Dark, swirling storm clouds spiraled above and beyond the ledge, giving the entire hill a spooky, purple-gray cast. The sharp, rocky bluff jutted out into the sky, and a heavy wind lashed menacingly at the clumps of small trees and shrubs that grew at the bottom portion of the hill.

The thick brush we were walking through gave way to the untended meadow. A gust of heavy wind swept the long grass blades, pushing them down, twisting them to and fro.

We were walking in a straight, single file line. Lyle Haywood, followed by Holly O'Mara, then myself. Shane Mitchell was behind me, then Dylan Bunker, and Tony Gritter brought up the rear. The wet grass crushed beneath our feet, leaving behind a line through the field to show where we'd walked.

I wasn't paying too much attention, just walking along behind Holly, every once in a while glancing up at the rock ledge jutting out from the top of Devil's Ridge. Actually, no one in the club was paying a whole lot of attention. We were just kind of moseying along, taking our time.

And then Lyle Haywood fell.

3

I heard a loud *thump* in front of me, and I heard Holly gasp. I turned.

Lyle Haywood had fallen flat on his face, spread eagle in the wet grass.

"Ow!" he yelled, wincing in pain. His shout was muffled by the fact that his mouth was planted squarely on the ground, in the grass. He rolled to his side, groaning, drawing his knee to his chest, holding the shin of his right leg with both hands.

"Nice going, you clod," Shane Mitchell scolded from behind me.

"Hey!" Holly O'Mara exclaimed, and she suddenly knelt down on one knee. "Look at this!"

I walked around Holly and looked down. Lyle was still

on the ground, grasping his shin, but he was slowly getting to his feet. Shane Mitchell suddenly appeared at my side, then Tony and Dylan, and we all stood around Holly, gazing down at an old, gray tombstone.

"That's cool!" Dylan Bunker said, nearly shouting.

"That's a heck of a place for one of those," Lyle grimaced. He was still holding his leg. I imagine he smacked his shin pretty good.

"What's a tombstone doing all the way out here?" Shane Mitchell wondered aloud.

I looked around, my eyes searching between the tall blades of grass. Not far away, I spotted something dark.

"There's another one!" I blurted out, pointing. I took a few steps toward the object, and, sure enough, it was *another* tombstone. The letters carved in it were old and worn, and it was obvious that the grave marker had been there a long, long time.

The group spread out, each of us searching for more. We discovered dozens of them, and they weren't hard to find, now that we knew that they were there. It was easy to see how they would have remained hidden, though. The unkept grass had grown up tall, concealing all of the tombstones from view. Even if you were standing at the edge of the field, you wouldn't be able to see any sign of the old graveyard. In fact, if we would have taken the trail through the evergreens, we'd have never come across them. With the tall grass growing up and around them, they were perfectly hidden from view.

Some of the grave markers were small, cylinder-shaped stones, yet others were quite large. I found one that was

nearly three feet tall and three feet wide. All of the headstones were made of solid rock, and all were very weathered. Some had dark, charcoal-colored stains running down them. Others had deep, jagged cracks. A few of the stones had started to disintegrate, and pieces had fallen to the ground.

"It sure is an *old* graveyard," Tony Gritter said, crouching low in the grass. "Look at this stone. It says that this guy was born in 1802, and he died in 1859."

"This one says 1842 is when this person died," Shane said, kneeling in front of a stone a few feet away from Tony.

We'd done a bit of walking around, and now, the wet grass was beaten down quite a bit, making the old cemetery more visible. We counted nearly fifty graves in all.

"Strange," Lyle Haywood contemplated, stroking his chin. "I don't ever remember hearing about a graveyard out here. I don't think I've ever seen it on the county map."

"This is cool," I said, looking around. Above, the boiling storm clouds gave the field a darkened, foreboding shade.

"It's kind of spooky," Dylan Bunker said, turning his head and scanning the grassland around us. "We're standing on a bunch of dead people."

"What do they care?" Tony Gritter said. "They're six feet underground. I'm sure they'll forgive you. Just don't stomp too hard." Holly O'Mara giggled. Shane and I laughed, too.

We spent a few minutes going from stone to stone, reading the names. Some we could read without any problem, others were so worn we could barely make them out. I recognized a few last names on the graves and wondered if they might be old relatives of some of the people I knew in Great Bear Heart.

Finally, Lyle began to walk toward the sloping hill that led up to the ridge.

"Come on," he said, looking up into the gloomy sky. "It's going to start raining again. Soon."

We hiked up the hill that rose up to Devil's Ridge. The embankment is quite a bit steeper than it looks, and we all had to lean forward and grab hunks of grass to keep us from losing our footing.

The farther we climbed, the harder it became. Soon, there was nothing to grab hold of but rock. I lost my grip once, and almost tumbled down the hill.

After we reached the top of Devil's Ridge, it didn't take us very long to find where the mouth of the tunnel was. It was right where Shane thought we would find it—tucked away beneath the rock cliff of the ridge. Because of the shadow of the ledge, the mouth of the tunnel was nearly invisible from below.

The six of us sprawled out flat on our stomachs, peering over the edge of the cliff, looking down. We weren't really that high in the air, maybe just up over the treetops, but we sure had a good view of our surroundings.

Directly below us in the rock cliff was the mouth of the tunnel. It sure wasn't very big—maybe two feet in diameter. Certainly not big enough for any of us to get into. Plus, it would have been difficult just to get to it. We'd have to climb down using a rope, suspended in the air, and then try and squirm in. One look at the tunnel told us that we wouldn't be going in there at all.

Not that we'd want to, either. The bat episode was still fresh in our minds, and I don't think that any of us wanted to get stuck in a tunnel when those little brown buggers came pouring out of there!

But I couldn't help but feel a bit disappointed. I was really hoping that, somehow, we would have been able to get into the tunnel. I was hoping that we would find the chest of silver dollars.

But, then again, there was no way any chest was hidden at this end of the tunnel. The opening was much too small.

"So that's it," Holly said softly, staring down at the gaping black cavity.

"I thought it would be harder to find," I said. "I figured that it couldn't be this easy."

"Some adventure this turned out to be," Tony Gritter said with more than a hint of disgust.

"Did you think we were going to find a pot of gold, or something?" Shane Mitchell asked.

"No," Tony Gritter replied. "But a chest full of silver dollars would have been pretty cool."

"Hey, it wasn't a total loss," Lyle Haywood replied. "I almost broke my leg on a gravestone. That has to be worth something." He rubbed his shin with his hand.

The six of us lay on our stomachs, looking down at the rock wall below us.

Suddenly, out of the corner of my eye, I saw something move. It drew my attention away from the tunnel, and I snapped my head around.

It was in the cemetery. Something in the graveyard had moved, I was sure of it.

And that's when things started to get real interesting.

4

"Did anybody see that?" I asked, my eyes scanning the graveyard at the bottom of the hill. Everyone turned their heads to see what I was looking at.

"See what?" Shane replied doubtfully.

"Something moved down there," I remarked, pointing. "In the graveyard."

We stared down at the gray headstones in the grass for a moment. From where we were on Devil's Ridge, the old cemetery was plainly visible. The tall, rain-soaked grass tossed wildly in the wind, and the surrounding trees shook with every gust. The sky above was dark and dreadful.

But nothing moved in the graveyard.

"I think you need to get your eyes fixed," Dylan said. "I don't see nothin'."

"I'm telling you, I saw something move down there," I reiterated.

"What did it look like?" Holly asked. The wind was tossing her hair about, and she reached out and pulled a lock from her face.

"I'm not really sure," I answered. "I just caught the flicker of a movement out of the corner of my eye."

"Probably just a bird," Lyle Haywood suggested, getting to his feet.

"No," I replied, shaking my head. "It wasn't a bird. I guess, well . . . maybe . . . maybe it was nothing." My eyes continued to search the graveyard for signs of movement. Still nothing.

A raindrop smacked hard into my cheek. Then another one hit my shoulder.

"Crud," Shane said, looking up at the sky. "I knew it was going to rain." He stood up, and Tony, Holly, and Dylan did the same. The wind picked up, and swollen storm clouds boiled overhead. We started carefully, but quickly, down the steep ridge.

When we were half way down the hill the clouds opened up, and rain came down in buckets. It poured and poured. Thunder rumbled menacingly from above, and a bright flash of lightning tore the sky open like a white-hot, jagged blade.

"Maybe this trip wasn't such a good idea after all," Tony Gritter shouted over the raging storm.

"Yeah, like a little rain is going to make you melt," Holly chortled.

"Well, Miss Smarty-Pants," Tony sneered. "I'm not really concerned about the rain. But one of those lightning bolts could really mess up my day."

We made it to the bottom of the ridge and began walking hurriedly through the old graveyard.

Suddenly, Dylan Bunker let out a piercing shriek. He was right in front of me, and he must've jumped two feet in the air! His arm snapped out, pointing at one of the larger gravestones.

Something had moved!

This time, we all saw it. We stopped dead in our tracks, the rain pounding at our soaked clothing. The wind howled, tossing the grass in all directions.

But there was no mistake. Something had moved behind the big grave marker. There was something hiding on the other side of the tombstone.

5

Not one of us moved. We all saw the movement, and no one wanted to be the first to investigate. I think we were all really scared. I know I was.

Not quite as scared as the time we had been in the submarine, but almost.

After a few seconds, Holly O'Mara got brave. She took a step toward the stone, slowly, ever so slowly, leaning sideways to peer around the huge grave marker. All at once her hands went to her hips, and a look of anger came over her.

"You!" she suddenly shouted. She took two big steps toward the gravestone and stopped. "What are YOU doing here?!?!?" she demanded.

At once, Larry Martin snapped up from behind the

stone, his white T-shirt soaked and clinging to his skin. His jeans were also soaked, and he had big black splotches on his knees from crouching down in the mud. Rain ran down his cheeks, and he had an arrogant smirk on his face that I wanted to smack off of him.

"Hey, it's a free country," he said snidely. "This is public property. I have just as much right to be here as you."

"Yeah, well, with all this 'free country' as you call it," Shane Mitchell retorted, "why did you have to pick a place where *we* were?"

"I was just out for a morning walk," Larry said slyly. "You know . . . get some fresh air, and take in the beauty of a summer rainstorm."

Yeah, right, I thought.

"Don't make me puke," Holly O'Mara said.

"Well, if you do puke," Larry Martin said, "make sure you clean it up." He looked around the old cemetery. "I think me and Gary and Terry are going to go camping here, and I don't want your barf all over the place."

"Camping?!?!" Lyle Haywood exclaimed. "You and your brothers? I think *I'm* the one that's going to puke."

"Stuff it, you skinny little shrimp," Larry snarled.

Shane Mitchell immediately came to Lyle's defense. "Why don't you just go somewhere else?" he asked.

"Yeah, like, take a long walk off a short pier," Dylan Bunker chimed.

Larry took a step forward and gave Dylan Bunker a shove. The situation was getting worse.

Larry Martin is older than we are, and a bit bigger. I don't think any one of us wanted to get into a fight with him, but I don't think Larry really wanted to get into a scrap, either. There were six of us, and only one of him.

"Let's go," Shane suddenly said, shooting Larry a nasty glance. I think Shane wanted to diffuse the situation before it got out of hand.

"That's a good idea," Larry said. "It's getting a little stuffy around here. You guys are starting to spoil my morning stroll."

Without any more words spoken, we turned and set off through the tall grass and back onto the trail. It was still pouring, and we all felt like drowned rats. Plus, we were all fuming mad with Larry Martin.

"Have a nice walk!" he shouted from behind us. "It's a GREAT day for a nice, long, hike!"

None of us turned to look at him. We were so mad, we were *steaming.*

"Man, would I just like to pound him," I said angrily. I made a fist with my right hand and slammed it into my opposite palm. "Just once. Just once I'd like to see him get what he has coming to him."

"Me too," Dylan Bunker agreed.

"Nobody's going to pound anybody," Shane Mitchell stated flatly. "All it'll do is get us into trouble."

He was right, of course. Any confrontation we had with the Martin's would just cause more problems. We certainly didn't need any help getting into trouble. Seems like we could always find it on our own.

We trudged along the path through the downpour. Rain fell through the trees, creating big droplets that, when they hit us, felt like wet marbles. The rain was steady, but at least the tumultuous thunder and lightning had stopped.

In a few minutes we had arrived at the place where we had left our bicycles—but we were in for a surprise.

And it wasn't a very good one.

I noticed it first. I stood my bike up and hopped on, but when I put my foot to the pedal, it was loose. There was no resistance when I placed my foot on the pedal. I looked down.

The chain was off! Not only that, but both of my tires were flat!

"Aw, for crying out loud," I said in disgust. I was about to tell everyone what happened, when Holly O'Mara spoke up.

"Hey!" she cried out. "My chain is off my bike! And my tires are flat!"

It was true. Not only was it true for Holly's bike as well as my own, but *all* of our bikes had flat tires, and *all* of the chains had been popped off!

We were boiling with rage. I was so mad, I wanted to run back to the old cemetery and find Larry Martin right then and there. He was behind this; there was no doubt about it. This is what he had meant when he yelled for us to *'have a nice walk'* when we were leaving the old cemetery. He knew that all of us would be walking all the way home . . . because he had flattened our tires and popped the chains off!

If we were mad when we left Larry at the cemetery, we were *fuming* now. Larry Martin hadn't done anything destructive to the bikes . . . he'd just unscrewed the valves on our tires and let all of the air out. Sure, the chains would go back on easy enough . . .but we would still have to push our bikes back to the clubhouse, and in the pouring rain, to boot.

We were silent as we pushed our bikes along Great Bear Heart Mail Route road. Not one of us said a single word.

Just when we were coming in to town, we saw the three Martin brothers sitting on the porch of their house. Larry had probably taken another trail through the woods and beat us back to Great Bear Heart. All three brothers soaking wet, and they looked like the cat had dragged them in from somewhere.

"Have a nice walk?" Gary asked. He giggled after he

spoke.

"Yeah, thanks to you!" Holly O'Mara fired back. Holly can get pretty feisty. I sure wouldn't want to be on her bad side when she wasn't having a good day.

The rest of us ignored Gary's comment. I think we were all so angry that we were about to explode, and it would be better just to keep our mouths shut for the time being.

It was apparent now that all three brothers had been behind the bicycle prank. They had probably been in the woods, watching the whole thing, chuckling to themselves about how they'd pulled a fast one on us.

And that's how we decided that we had to get back at the Martin brothers. For the time being, we would forget about the chest of silver dollars. Perhaps it was buried somewhere, or maybe it had been tossed into the lake. The possibilities were endless. We decided to suspend our search for the stolen loot and concentrate our efforts on Gary, Larry, and Terry Martin. No more games, no more holding back.

This was *war*. Total war.

7

The rain stopped later in the day, and the sun came out. We held a meeting in our clubhouse that evening to decide what to do.

"I say we go do the same thing to them!" Dylan Bunker declared, his eyes bulging with fury. "Let's go over to their house tonight and let the air out of their bike tires!" His cheeks were flush red. Dylan had taken the bicycle incident very personal. I don't think I've ever seen him so upset.

"Not good enough," Lyle Haywood said, shaking his head. "We have to *really* get back at them."

We tossed ideas around for more than an hour. Some of the ideas were pretty good, but they were either too destructive or would cost too much money to implement. Some ideas we had were just downright nasty. They sounded good at the time, but we weren't going to do anything that would get the Martin's hurt, or get us into trouble.

Dylan Bunker and Lyle Haywood were chattering about something, and Tony Gritter was walking to Holly O'Mara. Both Shane and I were just listening, catching bits and pieces of the two conversations. My eyes drifted to a shelf on the wall, and I spotted our two-way radios. We had bought them last year with money we had from our monthly club dues.

And all of a sudden, I had an idea.

A *good* idea.

Tony, Lyle, Holly and Dylan were still talking to one another. I leaned toward Shane, motioning him to lean closer. I whispered my idea to him, and, as I explained, a smile grew on his face. I could see the excitement blooming in his eyes.

"That's it!" he cried in jubilation, causing everyone else to stop talking. He turned to me. "Parker, you're a genius! It's perfect! Oh, man! That'll be great!" He started hopping up and down, doing a little bounce-type dance. I don't think I've ever seen Shane Mitchell so excited. "Tell'em!" he said, nodding at me. "Go ahead! Tell'em your idea!"

So, I did—and that's how the Adventure Club got into

the ghost business.

8

Our plan began simple, but soon, grew very complex.

Larry Martin had said that he and his brothers were going to go camping at the old cemetery at Devil's Ridge. I thought it might be fun if they had a few 'surprises' waiting for them.

My idea was to rig up a speaker and hide it behind one of the gravestones. One or two of us could hide in the woods and, after dark, when the Martin brothers were in their tent, we cold make weird whispers and noises into the radio. That would freak them out for sure!

But our 'simple plan' grew rather quickly. Shane decided that, since it was *such* a good idea to scare the pants off not one, but all the Martin's, that we should really go all-out.

He didn't want to just scare them . . . he wanted to petrify them. He wanted to horrify them. We *all* did. We wanted nothing more than to make the Martin brothers run, screaming and yelling at the top of their lungs, from the cemetery.

And man, we put the plan into high-gear.

We decided that our two-way radios weren't going to do the job. Besides . . . we were going to need them for our own communication between ourselves. No, Shane had a better idea.

His dad has an old stereo in the basement of his house, including two big speakers. Matter of fact, the speakers were about the size of gravestones—and that's what we made them look like.

Holly O'Mara is a whiz at pottery and crafts and things like that, and she put paper mache over the speaker boxes. While the mix was still drying, she rolled both of the boxes in sand. The sand gave the speaker boxes a gritty, rough look. Two days later, when the paper mache had dried, she spray-painted both speaker boxes gray. She even added few black streaks to make them look old.

When she finished, the two speakers looked *exactly* like big headstones . . . except they had speakers in them. Lyle Haywood connected the wires and ran them both to a small radio receiver that he borrowed from his dad.

But the real crowning glory was a sound-effects machine that Shane Mitchell's older brother had. It wasn't a very good one, but it was used to raise or lower the pitch of a voice, when a microphone was plugged into it. Shane played around with it at his house, then called us all to come over for a demonstration. We gathered in his basement.

"Okay," he said, grinning. "Listen." He had a cheap microphone plugged into the sound-effects generator. The sound-effects generator was plugged into a radio transmitter, which would be picked up by the receiver, which was connected to the speakers . . . speakers that looked like gravestones.

Shane spoke into the microphone. "Test, test, testing 1-2-3," he said. His voice came through the speakers, sounding just like Shane. It was a bit muffled from the speakers being covered with paper mache, but it sounded good.

"But that sounds like *you,"* Dylan Bunker spoke up. "They're going to know it's you right away."

"Just listen," Shane said confidently. He flipped a switch on the sound-effects generator and looked at us. A wide, mischievous grin grew on his face. Holding the microphone to his lips, he spoke.

"Get out of here!" he said. He spoke in a normal

voice, but when it came out of the speakers, his voice was anything *but* normal! It sounded deep and sinister, and didn't resemble Shane Mitchell's voice at all. Holly O'Mara jumped, surprised by the sudden change in his speech.

"That's *awesome!"* I exclaimed.

"GET OUT NOW!" Shane hissed menacingly into the microphone. His voice over the speakers was enough to make you want to run and hide.

Tony slapped Shane on the back. "Great job!" he said. "That's too cool! You're going to scare the living—"

"Shane!" a voice shouted from upstairs. *"Keep it down!"*

"Sorry, Mom," Shane hollered back. He killed the power on the transmitter and the sound effects generator, and placed the microphone on the table. The demonstration was over.

But we had a few more tricks up our sleeves. Operation 'Ghost in the Graveyard' as we called it, was going to include a show-stopping, heart-pounding prank. We were going to make sure we got the Martin's for good.

9

Tony Gritter's mom works at *Sigbey's*, which is a women's clothing store in Indian River, a city about four miles south of the town of Great Bear Heart. The small store uses mannequins—dummies—to display clothing. One day, Tony noticed one of the mannequins in the dumpster out behind the store. Apparently, the mannequin's hand was broken, and the store manager decided to toss the whole dummy out, thinking it was worthless.

Not anymore, Tony thought.

Later that evening, he rode all the way to Indian River on his bicycle, strapped the mannequin to the handlebars, and rode home. He was thirty minutes late for our weekly meeting because of it.

"Guys," he said frantically, popping his head through the trap door in the floor of our clubhouse. "Check this out!"

He climbed into the clubhouse and began pulling a rope up through the trap door. We could hear something below the clubhouse, banging through the branches. Then a white shape came up through the square hole in the floor. "Think this'll work?" he asked proudly. He was beaming as he proudly displayed his creation. "Ladies and gentlemen of the Adventure Club," he announced, "meet Homer."

It was the mannequin—sort of.

Tony had taken a white bed sheet and draped it around its head and body. The mannequin had no face, but it looked pretty spooky.

"And watch," Tony said. He reached beneath the sheet and raised the mannequin's arms, spreading them out. I have to admit, for a dummy, it sure looked a lot like a ghost!

"Why did you name him 'Homer'?" Holly O'Mara asked.

"Beats me," Tony Gritter shrugged. "I just thought that he looked like a Homer."

"Well, he looks great," Shane Mitchell began. He had a look of concern on his face. "But what are we going to do with him?"

Tony's smile grew, and his eyes burned with excitement. "We'll run a long wire from the top of Devil's Ridge to a tree on the other side of the cemetery," he said. "After the Martin's hear the voice through the speakers, they'll come out of their tent, right? It'll be dark, and they won't be able to see real well, even if they have flashlights. And they certainly won't be able to see all the way up to the top of the ridge. One of us will be there, and when they come out of their tent to investigate the voice from the speakers, all we have to do is hook Homer to the wire and let him fly! From where they'll be camping, it'll look like this thing is flying through the air—coming right at them!"

"Yes!" Lyle Haywood exclaimed.

"That'll be great!" Holly O'Mara chimed in.

"But hang on," Tony continued, his smile widening. "It gets better." He reached his hand behind the dummy's head. Suddenly, two glaring red eyes began to glow beneath the white material. They blinked on and off like two traffic lights. It was a pretty chilling effect.

"They're just two red lights connected to two 'D' cell batteries," Tony explained. "I cut out part of Homer's head and stuck the batteries inside. All you have to do is flick a switch, and they turn on."

The whole club let out a cheer, and Tony took a few

proud bows.

"No applause, no applause," he said merrily. He took a bow and bent forward, then back up. "Just throw money! Lots of money!"

We laughed and laughed. Our plan was set, and all we needed to do was get everything ready. We didn't know exactly when the Martin's were going to go camping in the old cemetery, but when they did, we'd be ready. Larry, Gary, and Terry Martin had no idea what they were in for.

10

The Martin's didn't go camping for another two weeks, and for those of us in the Adventure Club, they were two weeks of torture. We had no idea when the Martin's were going to go camping, and the waiting drove all of us bonkers.

Then one day Tony Gritter came scrambling up the rope ladder into the clubhouse.

"Dudes!" he said, out of breath, flinging the trap door open. He was huffing and puffing from running here all the way from town. "The Martin brothers!" he gasped, out of breath. "They're going camping! *Tonight!*"

"What?!?!" I exclaimed. "Are you sure?!?!"

"I was down at the hardware store," he said, collapsing onto a blue plastic milk crate. His chest heaved in and out. "While I was over in the paint section, Gary Martin came in. He didn't see me. He told Mr. Farnell that he needed some supplies, because he and his brothers were going camping tonight . . . at Devil's Ridge!"

Yes! This was what we'd been waiting for. We'd waited so long, we started thinking that maybe the Martin's weren't going to go camping. We thought that maybe Larry Martin had been full of hot air, and hadn't really meant to go camping in the old graveyard, after all.

Shane Mitchell sprang up from the milk crate he was seated on. "Quick!" he said. "We don't have any time to waste!"

We had a quick round-table discussion as to who was going to do what. Since we'd already had to wait two weeks, we pretty much had a grasp on what we were going to do, and how we were going to do it.

Now, it was going to happen. It was *really* going to happen, and it was going to happen *tonight.*

The haunting of the old graveyard at Devil's Ridge was about begin.

11

To say that we worked double-time that afternoon would be an understatement. We worked *triple*-time. We worked *quadruple*-time. Let me tell you, haunting an old cemetery is no small project.

Holly O'Mara and I had the job of somehow getting the speakers—gravestones—out to the site, which was no easy task. They were heavy. We had to put them in my old *Radio Flyer* wagon, and pull it behind my bicycle. Then we hid our bikes in some brush near the power lines, and pulled the wagon through the woods. Upon arriving at the old graveyard, we wasted no time setting up the speakers.

They looked great. The tall, slender grass camouflaged the two 'gravestones' perfectly. You'd really have to look close to determine that they were fakes.

We ran the speaker wires around other tombstones, through the meadow, and down to the edge of the evergreens, just as Shane had instructed. That was where he was going to place the receiver and the sound-effects generator. Since the transmitter wasn't very powerful, Shane would have to be pretty close to the electrical apparatus, yet far enough away that he wouldn't be spotted by the Martin brothers. The thick evergreen plot would provide ample cover.

Holly and I finished setting up just after five o'clock. Everyone else arrived a few minutes later.

Everyone had a job to do before we could take our places. Dylan Bunker stood watch from the trail, and would alert us if he saw the Martin's coming. Shane Mitchell hooked up the receiver, then hid in the woods with the microphone and ran some tests. Lyle Haywood and Tony Gritter brought Homer to the graveyard, hauled him to the top of Devil's Ridge, and made sure that he would slide down the wire properly. The wire had to run from the ridge to a tree on the other side of the graveyard, and we had to make sure that the angle wasn't too steep or too flat. The idea was to make the mannequin travel slowly and evenly down the wire for maximum 'scare' effect.

We worked frantically, always looking over our shoulder to make sure the Martin's weren't watching us.

Then, after we had set everything up and ran our tests, we had to wait. We waited and waited, hidden away in the thick forest surrounding the old graveyard. The sun began to sink into the trees as night began to fall. Crickets began to chirp from the field, and mosquitos buzzed around us. One of them nailed me right below my ear, and I wished I had brought some bug spray.

It grew darker, and we began to think that the Martin's weren't going to show.

Until we heard laughter coming from the trail near the power lines.

12

This was our plan:

We would wait while the Martin brothers set up camp, and went to bed. Shane Mitchell and Lyle Haywood were hiding in the evergreens with the microphone, and Dylan Bunker and Tony Gritter would stand-by in the swamp. Tony had one of the two-way radios, and when Shane gave him the all-okay, he and Dylan would climb Devil's Ridge from the other side, where they would be in charge of releasing Homer down the wire. Holly and myself remained right at the edge of the swamp, where we could see what was going on, but still remain hidden. From our hiding place, we had a perfect view of the graveyard, as well as Devil's Ridge.

The Martin brothers set up their tent on the edge of the

old cemetery, and proceeded to build an enormous bonfire. Terry had gone into the woods to hunt for wood, and we had a couple nervous minutes when he came pretty close to Holly and I. We froze, huddled beneath a thick alder. Terry Martin came within a few feet, but he didn't spot us.

"That was close," I whispered to Holly. She nodded in agreement, raising her eyebrows.

The night was dark, and thousands of stars twinkled in the sky above. Terry, Gary, and Larry Martin sat cross-legged around the fire. They were loud and obnoxious, and their uproarious laughter echoed through the dark night. It was no wonder that all three of them had been kicked out of the Boy Scouts.

Not long after dark, the fire began to fade. The three glowing forms of the three brothers became faint as the flames dwindled. After a while, the only thing left of the fire was a pile of glowing orange embers.

The campsite grew quiet. The night air was chilly, but not uncomfortable. Unseen crickets chirped all around us. Somewhere, a single, lonely owl hooted. Peeper frogs in the swamp on the other side of the ridge serenaded the darkness, their shrill songs pulsating like a high-pitched motor.

The Martins had gone to bed—and the fun was about to begin.

13

"When do you think Shane is going to say something?" Holly O'Mara whispered quietly.

"I'm not sure," I replied. *"I think he wants to wait until the Martins are asleep."*

We waited impatiently in the darkness, and the suspense was maddening. We didn't have a two-way radio, so we had no idea what was going on. Maybe the whole thing had been called off, and we didn't know about it. It sure seemed like we had been waiting a long, long time.

Suddenly, a strange, booming voice echoed over the graveyard. It was so eerie and spooky that I thought that it *couldn't* be Shane Mitchell. It was pitched lower than Shane's voice, and the effect was unbelievable!

"WHY ARE YOU HERE?!?!?" the strange voice

demanded.

Yes! Things were about to get real interesting.

Instantly, a light clicked on in the Martin's tent. Holly and I heard the tent flap unzip, and a flashlight beam began sweeping across the cemetery. We could hear frantic whispering coming from the tent. The flashlight beam slowly swept toward us, and Holly and I both ducked down, crouching as low as we could to the ground. Thankfully, the beam went over our heads, and continued on. We hadn't been spotted.

The Martins remained in the tent, scouring the old graveyard, the trees, and the field in the beam of the flashlight. They were talking among themselves, but we couldn't understand what they were saying. After about five minutes, I heard the tent flap zip close. The flashlight clicked off.

After a few more minutes, the deep, throaty voice boomed out again.

"HOW DARE YOU DISTURB US!" it said, surprising both Holly O'Mara and myself. The voice was louder, and I could hear it echo through the forest and field. Shane was really pouring it on.

The light in the tent suddenly clicked to life, and the tent flap whizzed open again. The light beam burst forth, illuminating the tall grass in the graveyard. The Martins were talking loudly now, but I still couldn't make out what they were saying. All we could hear was the frantic hissing of their voices.

The tent flap flew back, and the brothers emerged from the tent.

"Who . . . who's there?" Gary Martin stammered. His voice was tense, and it echoed over the old cemetery. Shane waited a moment before responding.

"HOW DAAAAAAARE YOOOOOOUUUU!" the voice suddenly thundered over the field.

Terry Martin dived back into the tent in terror. The flashlight beam went crazy as Gary and Larry Martin stood their ground, trying to spot where the voice was coming from.

"This is going to be good," I whispered to Holly O'Mara.

The two brothers took a few slow, cautious steps forward. I could see their shadows behind the beam. The two were whispering to one another.

"GET OUT!" Shane's altered voice bellowed once again. Gary and Larry Martin were now in the middle of the cemetery, and the voice was so sudden and abrupt that they couldn't tell where it had come from.

The flashlight beam whirled around like a mad spotlight, illuminating treetops and branches, and then sweeping over the thick grass. Headstones flashed through the beam as the two brothers desperately tried to find out where the voice was coming from.

At the top of Devil's Ridge, Tony Gritter and Dylan Bunker waited impatiently. Moments before, Shane had radioed them, giving them the okay to climb the hill. Tony and Dylan scrambled like little squirrels, hastily making their way to the north side of the rock ledge. From there, they had a perfect vantage point to see what was going on in the old cemetery.

Tony peered down into the graveyard below and whispered into the two-way radio.

"Okay . . . two of them are out in the graveyard. One is back in the tent. It's a 'go' for Homer." He let his finger off the microphone key.

"Whenever you're ready," Shane's voice cracked quietly over the radio. *"I'll wait for your cue."*

The delivery wire was tied to a tree on the far side of the cemetery. Tony Gritter leaned toward the ledge. He and Dylan had to lift the dummy over the cliff, hang it on the wire, and hold onto it until they were ready. Once, they almost dropped it.

"Okay, we're all set," Tony whispered into the two-way radio. *"I'm lettin'er fly in three . . . two—"*

He paused for just an instant, clicked on the glowing,

red eyes, and gave Homer a gentle shove.

"—one! There he goes!"

The mannequin began slowly descending down the wire. Suddenly, Shane's haunting voice boomed forth. It was louder this time, even more intense than before.

"YOU HAVE BEEN WARNED! NOW, I'M COMING FOR YOOOOUUUU!"

Holly and I sat huddled in the bushes, and we watched as holy terror broke loose in the graveyard. The flashlight beam suddenly swept upward, illuminating the white form of the dummy as it began to descend from the ridge.

It was *perfect!* The wire that was supporting the mannequin couldn't be seen, and Homer seemed to hover in the air, slowly coming down, right toward the Martin's camp! The red eyes blinked ominously, and the effect was hideous.

"PREPARE YOURSELVES!" the voice boomed out. *"THERE IS NO ESCAPE!"*

Gary and Larry Martin began screaming their heads off!

"Aaaaaaahhhhh!" one of the brother's screamed. "It's alive! It's *alive!"*

Pandemonium ensued as they both spun and made a mad dash for the tent—but they couldn't get in! The flap had been zipped shut by Terry! Gary and Larry went crashing into the nylon, yelling their heads off.

The flashlight beam whirled around, once again illuminating the ominous, white ghost above the cemetery. Homer was closer now, still descending down the wire, and his macabre, red eyes blinked dreadfully.

But the flashlight beam also lit up something else.

"Look!" Holly whispered, pointing up at the dummy. *"Look at that!"*

There was something else in the air . . . and in an instant, I knew what it was.

Bats! There were hundreds of them, swirling and swarming around the ghost. We could hear them now, fluttering wildy through the sky. Tiny squeaks and screeches began to fill the dark night, and, in the Martin's flashlight beam, the cloud of bats around Homer grew and grew.

"It's the tunnel!" I whispered. *"They must be coming from the tunnel beneath the rock ledge!"*

It made sense. The small tunnel opening in the rock ledge beneath the ridge stretched all the way back through Great Bear Heart to the library. We'd discovered the cavern of bats when we'd explored the tunnel. The narrow fissure beneath Devil's Ridge was how the bats came and went to the large cave beneath the ground, and, at night, the bats would leave their dark cave in search of food. The bats were harmless, and wouldn't bother the Martins, but the giant swarm of flying critters only added to the haunting sight in the sky.

Gary and Larry Martin began screeching in complete horror as the bats darted through the beam of the flashlight. The tiny creatures whizzed back and forth, to and fro, with lightning speed.

"Aaaaaaagggggghhhhhh!" the brothers screamed, flailing their arms madly above their heads. The tent had collapsed, and Terry Martin was flailing around inside, screaming in a mad panic. Gary and Larry desperately tried to get their brother out of the tent.

"Let's get out of here!" Gary shrieked, fumbling with the nylon tent. The tent flap suddenly zipped open, and we heard frantic scrambling as the Martins stumbled around in the darkness.

"Get the gear and let's split!" Larry shouted.

Yahoo! It worked! The Martins were finally getting what they deserved.

But there was on more incredible, stunning event that was about to happen. We didn't plan it—and if we had, we could have never planned for it to happen this perfectly.

And it happened the instant the guide wire snapped, sending Homer hurling to the ground.

14

The flashlight beam swung up in the air as the Martins began their getaway. Homer was moving faster now, sliding quickly along the wire, directly above the three brothers. For whatever reason—maybe the mannequin was just too heavy, or maybe there was a weak spot—but the wire broke in two.

When it snapped, the mannequin was almost directly above the Martin brothers. Homer suddenly plummeted, straight down—landing squarely on top of all three brothers!

The screams that they made were indescribable. They were yelling and wailing, their terrified voices echoing through the dark night. Their flashlight had gone out, and the only light came from the blinking of the gruesome, red eyes.

"AAAAHHH! HE'S GOT MEEEEE!" Larry Martin howled. *"He's got me! Get him off me! Get him off me! He's got meeeeeeee!"*

I thought I was going to explode. My stomach burned from holding my laughter in, and my ribs felt like they were going to bust wide open. Beside me in the darkness, Holly O'Mara held both of her hands tightly over her mouth to keep from giggling out loud. I could hear her choking back her laughter.

Branches crashed and broke as the Martin's made their frantic escape in the darkness. They were panicked, and they ran blindly through the forest, leaving their flashlight and all of their gear at the edge of the old graveyard. We could hear their frightened shouts and yells all the way to the power lines.

The haunting of the old cemetery at Devil's Ridge was a complete and total success.

15

After we were sure the Martin brothers were gone, Holly and I emerged from our hiding place in the brush. I clicked on my flashlight, and we met Lyle Haywood and Shane Mitchell in the middle of the old cemetery. Homer was on the ground, face down. His red eyes were still blinking madly, illuminating the blades of grass around his head. Lyle reached down and clicked the batteries off, and the blinking stopped.

"That was awesome!" I exclaimed.

"Did you see Gary and Terry fall into the tent?!?!" Shane asked, slapping his leg with his hand. "That was *funny!* It's going to be a long time before they ever go camping again . . . especially here at Devil's Ridge!"

Tony Gritter and Dylan Bunker came trudging through

the tall grass, swinging a lit flashlight.

"Did you see the bats?!?!" Dylan asked. "They came pouring out of the cave just a few seconds after we let Homer go!"

"We couldn't have planned it better!" Tony exclaimed proudly, slapping Dylan on the back. We all high-fived one another, and congratulated ourselves for a haunting well-done.

"That serves them right!" Holly O'Mara said. "After all the things they've done to us, it was about time we got'em back."

"Here, here!" I agreed. We were all laughing and talking so much among ourselves that we didn't hear the crunch of twigs approaching . . . until the dark shadow of a man suddenly appeared at the edge of the old graveyard.

16

Every hair on my body froze stiff. Not one of us spoke a word.

"Hello, over there," an old man's voice croaked. He sounded gentle and polite, and my fear subsided. We all relaxed a bit, but it was still strange that there was someone out here in the middle of the night.

Shane Mitchell shined his light over the cemetery, and we could see the old man. He was smiling, and he walked slowly toward us, weaving around the old gravestones.

"I thought I heard someone out here," he said. "You youngsters sure were making a racket."

"We . . . uh . . . we didn't think anyone lived near here," Lyle Haywood said.

"Oh, I don't live too far away." He turned, as if

peering into the dark forest. "Not far at all. Heard the commotion, and I just wanted to see what all the ruckus was about. It's hard for an old fella like myself to get much sleep with all this hubbub goin' on."

In the moonlight, I could see the old man clearly. He had a thick, handlebar mustache. Deep lines ran across his forehead, around his eyes, and down his cheeks. Straggly, shoulder-length gray hair covered his ears. His eyes were big and wide, but they were kind eyes. Caring eyes.

He looked at each one of us, then looked around. "The old Great Bear Heart cemetery," he said, focusing on one rather large headstone a few feet away. He crouched down, as if inspecting the stone. "I used to play out here when I was a young one, too. We all did. Then, something happened one night." He stood up and tilted his head back, staring up at Devil's Ridge. "Yup. Somethin' happened, and we never came back."

None of us said a word. All we heard were the crickets and peeper frogs.

"What . . . what happened?" Dylan asked.

The old man drew a breath and shook his head. "Well, now, I don't rightly know. But we saw . . . *something.* Standing here in the graveyard. Don't know what it was. Could have been a person, could have been a ghost. Scared us half to death."

None of us spoke, and the old man drew another breath.

"You kids run along, now," he said softly. "A graveyard is no place for young ones after dark. It's a place of rest. These folks here, they need their peace. You all have a good night."

Without another word, the old man turned and began to walk away. We could hear the swishing of branches and the breaking of twigs as he walked off into the darkness.

It was kind of weird, but I think we all felt like it was time to go. The old man was right . . . a graveyard probably wasn't the place to be hanging out after dark.

We packed up all of our gear in silence, and none of us said much to each other until we left the graveyard. Then we giggled all the way back to the clubhouse.

"You think that old guy was serious about seeing something in the graveyard?" I asked.

"Are you kidding?" Shane Mitchell replied. "He was just trying to scare us. You heard what he said. He doesn't live far from the cemetery. He just made up that story to scare us so we wouldn't come back and wake him up."

When I got home, I think I laughed myself to sleep, thinking about the Martins and how they really got what was coming to them.

But I couldn't help but wonder about what the old man

had said. What had he seen so long ago? Or was he simply making up the story, like Shane said?

Strange.

At the next meeting of the Adventure Club, it was Shane Mitchell who was late, which was really unusual.

"Maybe he forgot," Dylan Bunker reasoned. "I mean, shouldn't he be here by now?"

"Yeah, and you should talk," Tony Gritter chided. "You're the one who can't ever make it here on time."

Dylan Bunker stuck his tongue out and gave Tony a raspberry just as the trap door unexpectedly flew open. Shane Mitchell's head popped up, and he climbed into the clubhouse.

Instantly, we all knew something was wrong.

Really wrong.

Shane's face was white, and his eyes were huge. He held a picture frame in his hand. He closed the trap door in the floor.

"I found this down at the hardware store," he said quietly. His voice was stiff and tense. He held out the picture frame. "Be careful. I borrowed it from Mr. Farnell. I have to take it back to him."

We all gathered around Shane, and Holly took the picture from his hands. It was and old black-and-white picture, yellowed with age. Five men stood in front of a stringer of a dozen or so big fish, displaying their catch of the day.

"I don't get it," Lyle Haywood said.

Shane Mitchell reached out his hand, and placed his finger on the glass. Without a word, his finger found one of the men.

"Look familiar?" he said shakily. He was nervous and jittery. This was not at all like Shane Mitchell. He sounded like he was *scared.*

We all peered at the man Shane was pointing to.

"Oh my gosh!" Holly O'Mara suddenly gasped. "That's . . . that's—"

"—that's the guy in the graveyard!" I finished. "That's *him!"*

There was no mistake. The handlebar mustache, the thick lines on his forehead and face. It was him, all right.

"That's Artemus Culligan," Shane Mitchell explained, his voice still quivering.

"Big deal," Tony Gritter said. "So we know who he is. So what?"

Shane's answer sent a chill up my spine that I will never forget. He looked at each one of us, then looked at the picture in Holly's hands. "So, it just so happens that Artemus Culligan has been dead for fifty years," he said, his voice trembling. "Artemus Culligan died in 1951—and

I don't think I need to tell you where he's buried."

None of us in the Adventure Club ever again set foot in the old cemetery beneath Devil's Ridge.

Flight of the Falcon

1

When Holly O'Mara gets bored, she doodles. She'll pull out a paper and a pencil and just draw things, often for hours at a time. She'll sketch anything. Trees, cars, people. She's quite good, and we all think she's a pretty talented artist.

And that's what she was doing in our clubhouse on this particular day. It was a stifling hot afternoon in August, a few weeks before school started. August in Great Bear Heart can have some pretty hot days, mind you, and this day was a real steamer. It was one of those days when the humidity made your skin feel damp and sticky. There wasn't even the hint of a breeze, so our clubhouse was like an oven.

We'd been talking all summer, on and off, about

building some sort of airplane. Not some four-foot model that you could buy in a department store or hobby shop, but one that we could actually fly ourselves. Tony Gritter's dad gets a magazine called *Popular Mechanics,* gives them to Tony when he's done with them, and he brings them to the clubhouse. We all go through the periodical. Inside many of the magazines, among other things, are pictures of lightweight planes and gliders that people had designed and made themselves. There were even kits you could buy to build your own, but most cost a lot more money than the club had. We'd been racking our brains on a way to make some sort of airplane without spending every nickel we'd saved.

"I think we should build a really fast one," Dylan Bunker suggested, sweeping his hand across the air in front of him. "One that breaks the speed of sound!"

"Get real," Tony Gritter said. He frowned, and his forehead wrinkled like ripples on a pond. "That would take thousands and thousands of dollars. Maybe millions."

"Whatever we build," Lyle Haywood offered, "it'll have to be something light. Something that doesn't weigh very much."

We all had our own ideas of how the flying machine should be built, what materials it should be built out of, and how it would be powered. We had some good ideas, and some of them might have worked . . . if we had the money. But for the most part, our ideas were completely impractical. Nothing we'd sketched out or designed seemed like it would work.

Except for Holly O'Mara's drawing.

She'd been quiet during the meeting, pencil in hand, paper on her lap, doodling away. I just figured that she was bored and passing the time by scribbling away at something. Tony Gritter was sitting next to her, and he leaned over to see what she'd been drawing. His eyes suddenly got really big, and he snapped his fingers, then pointed to the pad of paper that Holly was drawing on.

"That's it!" he flared. "Holly . . . that's *brilliant!*" We all rushed around Holly to see what she had been drawing.

It was a glider . . . sort of. But as we looked at it more and more, we began to realize that, by golly, Holly's idea just might work!

What she'd drawn was kind of a hang glider, but it had been modified a bit. The canopy, or wing, was triangular. However, while most hang gliders are for a single person, Holly had replaced the single-man hang apparatus with a two-seat extension.

But perhaps what was most intriguing was that there was no motor, so to speak.

The machine Holly had designed was pedal-powered!

Holly had drawn two pairs of bicycle pedals, connected to chains that ran alongside the seats. The chains turned two sprockets that turned the blades of two large fans! The fans would power the machine like jet engines, and the two persons flying the contraption would pump the pedals to help keep the craft aloft. Holly had drawn the machine in-flight, with two people seated in the chair, pedaling away as the craft flew over the treetops. Beneath the drawing she'd scribbled one word:

Lyle Haywood picked up Holly's pad of paper and studied her drawing. Lyle has a knack for these things. After all, he was the one who had found the old research submarine in old man Franklin's junkyard, and he had been instrumental in re-building the engine with Shane. Lyle Haywood is probably one of the smartest people I know.

Lyle adjusted his glasses and studied the drawing, squinting at every detail. He placed his finger to the paper.

"This needs to be here," he said quietly to no one but himself. "And if we adjust the chain drive mechanism back a little bit . . . ."

Without even being asked, Holly O'Mara handed him her pencil. Lyle took it without removing his eyes from the sketch. He began making short scribbles and lines, changing this and that. Finally, he had finished.

"There," he said confidently. "*Falcon* just might fly. Great job, Holly."

He turned the sketch around for all of us to see. He'd made a few changes to the framework of the craft, but, all-in-all, it was true to form to Holly's original idea.

And it looked *cool!* Our excitement grew like an inflating balloon, expanding with every passing second.

"Anybody wanna vote on this?" Shane Mitchell asked.

"I move that we don't waste any time voting," Tony Gritter said. "We just go for it!"

"I second that motion!" I exclaimed, shooting my hand into the air.

And that was that. Without even voting, we'd opted to go ahead with the task of building the *Falcon.*

Alas, the Adventure Club has a certain flair for getting into big trouble . . . and this project was going to be no exception.

2

The great thing about the *Falcon* was that it wasn't going to cost us much money. The aluminum frame for the single wing, and all of the steel tubing for the seat, came from the junkyard. Old man Franklin gave us a pretty good deal, and he kicked in two old heavy-duty fans for free. They were kind of beat up, but they were made with sturdy, metal blades and steel casing. Mr. Franklin said that the motors didn't work and were beyond repair, but that was okay with us. It wasn't the motors we were interested in.

At a garage sale, Shane Mitchell found two very old ten-speed bikes. They were rusting, and the chains were missing. All of the tires were flat, but the pedals and sprockets were in decent enough shape. He bought both bikes for five bucks each. His older sister had just moved away to go to college, so he swiped the chain from her bicycle, and another from his mom's mountain bike. She hadn't been riding it much this summer, so Shane figured he could probably just 'borrow' the chain for a while.

The wing material was a problem. We needed something that would be strong enough to support the weight of two people, *and* the *Falcon* itself. In addition, it needed to be really lightweight. Holly, Tony and I spent hours going through Franklin's junkyard, but we didn't find anything. The only thing we found were old canvas tarps with holes chewed in them. Until we could find some suitable wing material, the construction of the *Falcon* was at a standstill.

At our next meeting, we discussed the problem.

"Can't we just use some heavy plastic sheeting?" Dylan Bunker pleaded. He was really anxious to keep the project moving, but, then again, so were all of us.

"Don't be a dork," Tony Gritter barked, shaking his head. "Plastic won't last two seconds. How would you like to be up in the air and have the whole thing tear apart?"

Dylan looked hurt, and Holly O'Mara came to his defense.

"It was just a suggestion," she snapped at Tony. "I don't hear any ideas coming from *you.*"

"Well, if we had any brains among us, we'd have this

problem fixed by now," Tony Gritter answered sharply. "Maybe we should all go and rent some intelligence or something."

I spoke up. "Maybe we should just—" but I stopped speaking when I saw the expression on Lyle Haywood's face.

"That's it!" he suddenly exclaimed. "Man . . . why didn't we think of that sooner!"

We were puzzled. "What?" Shane Mitchell asked. "Think of *what?"*

"Renting!" Lyle thundered, spreading his arms wide. "There's a place called *Express Rental* south of town that rents just about everything imaginable! When Great Bear Heart has the annual summer chicken barbeque, they rent tents from *Express Rental!* I'll bet they have nylon tents!"

"We can't rent a tent," I said. "We'd have to cut it up to fit our wing. If we did that, then we'd have to buy it. Tents like that are expensive. We don't have the money for that."

"Maybe not," Lyle agreed, "but I'll bet that they've got some old ones that are torn, and maybe they don't use anymore."

"I still think it's a long shot," I replied.

It wasn't.

As it turns out, Lyle Haywood was right on the money.

Express Rental didn't have the exact size nylon sheet that we needed, but it just so happened that they had two old tents that they didn't use anymore. One had a big tear in it, and the other had a hole right in the middle. Lyle bought both of them for ten dollars . . . the exact amount that Shane Mitchell had spent for the two bicycles.

Our parts list was complete, except for a few smaller odds and ends that we could pick up from the junkyard as we needed them.

Operation *Falcon* was under way.

3

We worked in a small, white cement building that's directly across from the hardware store. It used to be a filling station, but it's been closed for years. It's owned by Mr. Farnell, who also owns the hardware store, and he said we could use the old garage for whatever we wanted, as long as we cleaned up our mess.

Like our submarine project, we all had different things to do. Lyle Haywood and Holly O'Mara were unofficially in charge of overseeing the construction, going over plans, re-drawing, and making changes to the craft. Dylan Bunker and I were in charge of the pedal apparatus, and Shane Mitchell and Tony Gritter worked on creating a housing for the two big fans. We all worked with the wing, being that it was so big and cumbersome. Sewing the two pieces of the wing together was a project in itself, but after a few trying hours, we got the hang of it. Tony Gritter devised some nifty clamps that fastened the nylon wing to the frame apparatus, and they worked beautifully.

Dylan and I finished the pedal mechanism, and Shane and Lyle helped us affix it to the frame. The seats needed to be comfortable, but lightweight, so we nabbed a couple of folding lawn chairs from Shane's house. They were both different colors, and they looked kind of cheesy, but they would be perfect for what we needed them for. With the addition of some aluminum framing, and some wheels that we'd swiped from an old baby-buggy I found in Franklin's junkyard, the two seats began to look like a single cockpit.

It took some time to get the fans to operate properly in conjunction with the gears and sprockets, but after a bit of tweaking, we were able to adjust the ratio of blade rotations to a workable function. The whole idea, obviously, was that the faster you pedal, the faster the fan blades would rotate. Since the pedals weren't in any way connected to the three wheels, the fans would be the single source of propulsion.

We needed to try the cockpit without connecting the wing apparatus. We had to know if the two fans alone would be able to make the machine move with the weight of two people on board. Since Dylan Bunker and I were the ones to design and assemble the pedal mechanism, we were chosen to be the ground test-pilots.

Shane Mitchell opened the garage door, and we wheeled the contraption closer to the lake. There used to be an old railroad that ran along the shore, but the tracks have long since been pulled up. All that is left now is a sturdy trail used for hiking and biking. It would serve as a perfect test runway. Of course, there were too many trees and power lines around for our initial test flight, but we didn't have to worry about that now. We'd fly the *Falcon* from a safer location that was free of standing trees and other obstructions. Right now, all we needed was a straight, smooth pathway.

Seated in the cockpit was a lot like being seated in a paddle-boat, except we had a few more control levers. Dylan and I took our seats, and Shane gave us the all-clear.

"Let's go!" Dylan shouted, and we both began pumping our legs as fast as we could.

It worked like a charm! The fan blades began to spin, slowly at first, but picking up speed quickly. In no time at all, the cockpit began to lurch forward. It reminded me of one of those air boats that they use in the Florida everglades. The whirring fans on board were used to propel the boats over the marsh, because there are too many logs and submerged objects to have a propellor below the surface. The *Falcon* worked along that same principle.

"Pedal harder!" Holly O'Mara shouted from behind us.

"Yeah!" Shane boomed. "Give'er all you've got!"

Surprisingly, we were able to go quite fast. Our steering wasn't real great, since we only had a single lever to control the two front wheels, but we managed. Besides, the real steering would take place in the sky. The *Falcon* would have levers and flap adjustments for in-flight control.

Behind us, we could hear Holly, Lyle, Shane and Tony cheering. It was going to work! It was *really* going to work!

The four-wheeled cockpit whizzed down the old railroad bed, bouncing over rocks and clumps of grass. We traveled about a hundred feet at a pretty good clip.

"Okay, let's head back," I said, slowing my pumping legs. The cockpit came to an abrupt halt, and the whirring fan blades stopped. Behind us, a cloud of dust hung in the air above the trail. Dylan and I had to get out of our seats and physically turn the cockpit apparatus around, as the old railroad bed was quite narrow.

In seconds, we were off again. The ride was bouncy, but we hardly noticed. What we noticed was that it worked. The two pedal-powered fans pushed enough air from our feet to propel us over the ground.

"Rock and roll!" Lyle Haywood shouted as the unwinged cockpit rolled to a stop in front of the group. "It works!"

Dylan and I jumped out of the cockpit and the six of us rolled it back up to the garage. We were all talking excitedly about what a cool project this was. Everyone congratulated Holly O'Mara for coming up with such a brilliant idea.

Back in the garage, attaching the huge wing to the cockpit was no small task, by any means. It was big and awkward to work with, and it took all six of us to hold it up while Tony Gritter bolted the aluminum piping to the cockpit tubing. The process took nearly two hours, and by the time we were finished, we were exhausted.

The last thing we affixed were safety buckles. Dylan and I had found two seat belts from an old truck at Franklin's junkyard, and they worked great in the cockpit.

The *Falcon* was ready for flight.

The six of us stood around silently, our excitement bubbling beneath our skin. The *Falcon* looked *cool.* Oh, sure, she wasn't a beauty queen by any means. The aluminum piping was discolored, the pedals were different colors and didn't match, the control levers were blackened and scarred from being welded, and the nylon wing had a big seam across the top where we had to sew the two pieces together.

But she was *ours*. We'd built the *Falcon* from scratch for about fifty bucks total. I would go as far as to say that we *loved* the *Falcon,* each and every one of us.

Question was: would we still be able to pedal hard enough to achieve lift-off? We'd added a bit more weight with the fixed-wing apparatus, and pedaling the aircraft wouldn't be as easy as our initial test had been.

Was it possible? Would the *Falcon* really fly?

We'd find out soon enough.

4

The following morning, we all met at the garage at ten, sharp. Surprisingly, even Dylan Bunker was on time. No one wanted to be late for the test flight of the *Falcon.*

The day was sunny and hot, and a light breeze was blowing. The small town of Great Bear Heart was filled with the normal sights and sounds of summer: cars passing by on the highway, a few scattered people walking through the small park, and a half-dozen boaters on Puckett Lake, getting an early start on the day. The air was fresh, scented with just a hint of flowers. It was the perfect morning to take the *Falcon* out.

We decided that our initial test flight should take place on a dirt road that wound around McArdle's farm, near our clubhouse. There were no power lines or poles to interfere, and the trees were cut way back from both shoulders of the road. The only buildings nearby were Mr. McArdles's farm house and barn, but they were way over on the other side of the field. The dirt road dead-ended at a stand of towering oaks trees. But our make-do runway would be plenty wide, providing a broad area for the *Falcon* to take off and land.

At the garage across from the hardware store, we tied ropes to our bikes, then bound the other ends to the cockpit of the small plane. Lyle Haywood sat in the *Falcon* and steered the craft, and we hopped on our bikes and pulled the awkward contraption across the street, up past the hardware store, past both churches, up the hill, and out to McArdle's farm. I imagine that it looked pretty funny, the five of us pulling the strange invention through town and up the street. But we were persistent, and it only took us ten minutes to get to the deserted dirt road.

So far, the only problem we had was the fact that we *all* wanted to be the first test-pilots. I myself thought that I would make a good pilot, but then again, so did Tony Gritter. And Shane. And Holly, Lyle, and Dylan. We began arguing amongst ourselves as to who should be chosen to fly the *Falcon.*

"All right, all right," Shane Mitchell intervened. "Let's be sensible, here. There are only two people who are going to fly this craft. Someone who knows how to fly it, and the person whose idea it was in the first place."

Well, we all knew then and there that Lyle Haywood would be the pilot of the *Falcon,* since he had pretty much designed the final version of the craft and engineered all of the controls. Besides . . . Lyle had captained the ill-fated submarine, and had, in fact, saved our lives when the sub had sprang a leak. Holly O'Mara had been the one to actually come up with the original idea for the *Falcon*, so she would be the co-pilot.

It made sense, and we quit our arguing. I think that we were all so excited about the prospect of the *Falcon* actually *flying* that we got a bit caught up in ourselves. We settled down and began to prepare for the first voyage.

Lyle and Holly took their places and buckled themselves in.

Tony Gritter carried our two-way radios in his pack. He turned them both on, gave one to Holly, then walked away. After he'd gone a dozen yards or so, he stopped and turned around.

"Check, one, two three," he spoke into the radio. "Can you hear me?"

"Loud and clear," Holly acknowledged, keying the microphone and drawing the radio close to her lips.

I licked my finger and held it up in the air. The breeze was out of the west, and it was a smooth, gentle wind. The sky was blue, blotted here and there by big, white, puffy clouds. Conditions couldn't be better.

Shane had brought two snowmobile helmets. He handed one to Lyle, and one to Holly. Each strapped the helmets to their heads and gave Shane the thumbs-up. Holly's hair stuck out from the back and sides of her helmet, and Lyle's glasses made him look like a giant, skinny bug with his helmet on. They looked kind of funny in the middle of summer, each wearing black helmets that read *Polaris* on the side. But it was a necessary precaution to wear them—just in case the unthinkable happened.

And it was a good thing—because the unthinkable was about to happen, and there was nothing we could do to stop it.

5

An hour later, the moment of truth was at hand. We'd made all the preparations, and taken all of the precautions we could think of. Lyle Haywood and Holly O'Mara were seated firmly in the cockpit, awaiting the all-clear from Shane Mitchell. Finally, after he'd checked and re-checked the bolts and wires to make sure they were all secure, he nodded his head.

"She's all set," he said confidently.

Now, looking back, maybe I should have said something at that moment. During our preparations and double-checking, I noticed that the breeze had picked up. By the time we were ready for the first test-flight, the wind was gusting. However, from where we were on the road, the trees sheltered us from the wind, so we really had no idea just how windy it had become. I sensed a heavy breeze, but I thought that it would probably help the *Falcon* get off the ground.

Lyle Haywood held out his hand and Holly shook it. "Good luck," he said.

"I *really* hope you know how to fly this thing," Holly replied.

Tony and Shane each grabbed a side of the wing. When Lyle gave the signal, they would begin to run and help the craft along, which would give Holly and Lyle a bit of a boost during the take-off.

Lyle Haywood took a deep breath, looked at Holly, then turned to Shane Mitchell. He nodded his head and didn't say a word.

"Let's go!" Shane shouted, and he and Tony began to urge the craft along.

Holly and Lyle began pedaling, and soon the *Falcon* was taxiing down the dirt road. Moments later, it was going so fast that Shane and Tony couldn't keep up. They let go of the craft and stopped, watching the small plane speed down the gravel runway. The single wing bent and swayed as the craft bounced along the road.

"Faster!" I yelled. "Pedal harder! *Harder!"*

"Yeah!" Dylan Bunker encouraged. He jumped up and down, and threw his fists into the air. "Go, man, go!"

The *Falcon* was really moving now, but it hadn't left the ground.

"Come on, come on," Shane whispered.

The longer the *Falcon* continued along the dirt road, the more our hearts began to sink. Maybe the bird wouldn't lift off, after all.

Still, Lyle and Holly pumped their legs with all they had, and the *Falcon* sped down the gravel runway. The small aircraft creaked and squeaked as it bounced along on its baby-buggy wheels.

"Is this thing going to ever get off the ground?!?!" Holly O'Mara complained loudly.

"We aren't getting enough lift!" Lyle answered. "If we had just a bit more speed . . . ."

But they were pedaling as fast as they could. In a few moments, they'd have to stop at the end of the road.

We were all silent. The *Falcon* was a failure.

At least, it seemed like it at the time.

The dirt road that winds around McArdle's farm is surrounded by trees, cut about forty feet back from the shoulder. As the road begins to approach McArdle's field, the trees are clear-cut, giving way to an enormous field. On the other side of the field is where our clubhouse is.

When the *Falcon* reached the place where the trees fell away and the field opened up, the craft didn't just *leave* the ground . . . it rocketed right off the road and into the air so quickly that we were all left speechless! The *Falcon* shot upward so violently that we immediately sensed trouble. Serious trouble.

Suddenly, it made sense.

"The field!" I shouted. "There's a heavy wind blowing today! We just couldn't feel it because the trees blocked it!"

Dylan Bunker suddenly gasped, and his mouth hung open in terror. "Oh no!" he shouted, pointing.

The *Falcon* was still climbing upward, but it had clearly been caught up in the wind. It just barely made it over a large red pine, then almost hit another tree dead on! We could make out Holly and Lyle pedaling like mad, trying to regain control of the craft.

"It's too windy!" Tony Gritter shouted. "They can't control it! Come on!"

We hopped on our bikes and shot down the road in the direction of the wavering aircraft. Of course, there wasn't much we would be able to do here on the ground, but we didn't want to let the aircraft out of our sight, should something happen.

The *Falcon* had cleared the treetops, and now it looked like Lyle had gained a bit of control of the plane. Both he and Holly had steadied their pedaling, and the craft appeared to be turning back toward us.

Just ahead of me, Tony was on his bicycle, his legs pumping the pedals like pistons. He reached behind him and un-clipped the two-way radio from his belt, expertly steering his bike with one hand.

"Holly! Lyle! You guys okay?!?!?" He shouted into the radio.

High in the sky above, I could see Holly O'Mara draw her hand up to her mouth. She was holding the radio, and in the next instant, her voice boomed from Tony's hand-held.

"Yeah, we're okay," she replied. Even through the radio, I could hear her voice trembling with nervousness. "For a minute I thought we were going to hit those trees, but I think we've got it under control now."

We slowed our bikes and cruised to a stop, our heads tilted back and eyes to the sky, watching the *Falcon* in flight. It was magical.

"Yes!" Dylan Bunker said, thrusting his fist into the air. "I knew she would fly! I knew it!"

We watched as the small plane cruised over the field. It was bumping up and down a lot, and Holly and Lyle looked like they were really getting tossed around in the wind. It was a good thing we'd put those seat belts in the cockpit, that was for sure.

Lyle Haywood's radio squawked again, and Holly's voice crackled.

"Lyle says it's too windy up here," she explained. "We're coming back down."

I guess we were a bit disappointed that the flight would be over so soon, but, all in all, we were jubilant. The *Falcon* was flying! She was *really* flying!

We moved our bikes to the side of the road to give Lyle room to land the craft. After he'd made a big, wide turn, he leveled off, then began to slowly descend toward the road.

And that's when a really good day turned really, really bad.

6

Suddenly, a fierce gust of wind came out of nowhere, jolting the tiny plane sideways. The entire craft rolled violently to one side, and I was sure it was going to roll completely upside down! I saw Holly hit her helmet against an aluminum bar in the cockpit, but she looked like she was okay. Lyle was desperate at the controls, trying to right the *Falcon* before he lost all maneuverability.

On the ground, we weren't much help. There was nothing we could do but watch the *Falcon* tumble helplessly in the wind, tossed about by the furious gale.

And suddenly, to our horror, the craft *was* upside down! Another strong gust had forced the *Falcon* completely over. Lyle and Holly hung, inverted, held only by the old seat belts that fastened them in the cockpit. The craft began to spin, upside down. It was plummeting rapidly toward the earth. In a matter of seconds, the doomed *Falcon* would crash helplessly into the trees.

"Oh no!" I screamed. *"Holly! Lyle!"*

The four of us watched, horrified, unable to save our friends. In a matter of seconds, they would crash.

But the wind, which was still blowing mightily, gave the ill-fated craft—and Lyle and Holly—a second chance.

Another strong gust suddenly righted the plane, snapping it back over in one swift motion. The *Falcon* was no longer dropping as quickly as it had been, but it was still being wildly tossed about by the heavy wind. Lyle immediately tried to regain control, fumbling with levers, and adjusting wing flaps. The four of us on the ground breathed heavy sighs of relief.

"Holly!" Tony Gritter shouted into the two-way radio. *"Holly! You guys have to land that thing!"*

The radio sputtered and coughed. "We're trying!" Holly panicked. "But it's *really* windy now! Lyle is having a hard time regaining control!"

And in the next instant, another gust of wind had lifted the aircraft even higher into the sky . . . and over the treetops! The *Falcon* had disappeared from view, and the last thing we could hear over the radio was Holly's scream of complete terror.

7

We leapt into action.

The first thing we need to do was to find out if Lyle and Holly were all right. The four of us jumped on our bikes and headed down the road at breakneck speed.

"Holly!?!? Lyle!?!?" Tony screamed into the radio. *"Holly!?!? Lyle!?!?"*

There was no answer. The silence over the radio was confirming our worst fears, and terror grew within me like a monster. I couldn't bear to think what had happened.

"Over there!" Dylan pointed. There was a trail that cut off from the dirt road at about the place we'd last seen the *Falcon.* "This trail goes through the woods all the way down to the post office!"

We wound our bikes around trees, and splashed

through a small stream. Branches and limbs whirred by, scraping my face and smacking my shoulders.

"Holly!?!? Lyle!?!?" Tony pleaded into the radio again. *"Can you hear me?!?!?!?"*

There was still no answer from Holly or Lyle. The situation was desperate, to say the least, and we were preparing for the worst. Holly and Lyle had crashed. We were almost certain of it.

Suddenly, I caught a dark shape in the sky! It was a ways off, but I definitely knew what it was. My heart soared.

It was the *Falcon!*

"There they are!" I shouted, removing one hand from my handlebars and pointing. "Up there! They're still flying!"

Tony Gritter skidded his bike to a halt. Dylan Bunker was looking up into the sky and didn't see Tony stop, and he ran into the back of his bike. The impact sent Dylan sailing over his handlebars, tumbling headlong into the brush.

"Hey!" he sputtered, scrambling to his feet. "Watch what you're doing!"

Tony ignored him. He snapped the radio up to his mouth. "Holly! Lyle! Can you hear me?!?!?"

The radio cracked and popped, and Holly's voice came

across. "Yes, we're fine now, but we still don't have much control of this thing. The wind is just too strong. It's all we can do to keep steady and not let the wind roll us over. Lyle's not sure we can land this thing in this strong of wind. Uh-oh—hold on a second."

We waited impatiently for Holly's voice to return. Seconds clicked by, and then Lyle Haywood's voice came from the radio. He sounded serious and tense. Not at all the happy-go-lucky Lyle Haywood that we knew.

"Guys, we have a problem up here. When the plane flipped, it put too much strain on the wing. It looks like a couple of bolts are loose. One looks like it's about to break. I think it'll hold . . . but not for long."

We quickly realized we had a dangerous situation on our hands. Not only was the wind too strong for Lyle to get complete control of the plane, but now, the *Falcon* was damaged, and in danger of going down. The *Falcon* had to land immediately . . . but where? And where would they land, even if Lyle could get control of the craft? It would be hard enough to find a field or a road to put the craft down, even without the gusting winds.

Dylan brushed himself off, pulled a few picker balls out of his hair, and hopped back on his bicycle. The four of us took off once again. Tony held the radio in one hand.

"What's below you? Where are you?"

There was silence for a moment, and then Holly's voice crackled.

"We're almost directly above Great Bear Heart. Just a bit north."

I was mentally trying to picture the terrain beneath the *Falcon.* There wouldn't be many, if any, places to land the craft. And the wind was carrying the *Falcon* east, which would put them directly over Puckett Lake.

An apple formed in my throat as I thought of the consequences. If the *Falcon* went down in the lake, it would be all over for Holly and Lyle. Just the thought wrapped my stomach up in knots. It reminded me of the problems we had with our submarine, and how Lyle had barely made it out alive of the sunken *Independence*.

We had to think, and think fast. On the ground, there wasn't much we could do. We were totally at the mercy of the weather.

In the distance, I saw the plane take another unexpected uplift, climbing even higher. The wind was really taking the *Falcon* now.

"Okay," Holly O'Mara's voice sputtered over the radio. "We're directly over the town. The wind is carrying us over the lake."

Those were the words we didn't want to hear. If something happened, and the *Falcon* went down in Puckett

Lake, we'd never get to Holly and Lyle in time.

We rode our bikes down to the post office, our eyes gazing up into the sky as we traveled. High above, the *Falcon* was now only a tiny speck, and it was moving fast.

We crossed the highway and rode our bikes behind the library and into Puckett Park. The *Falcon* was really moving now, and was already half way across the lake! It looked like a big, fat, soaring eagle from where we were.

Suddenly the radio cracked, and Holly's voice came through. "Okay, okay, Lyle thinks he might have control," she said.

Our hearts leapt. Maybe this whole thing would have a happy ending, after all.

"You guys should see everything from up here!" Holly exclaimed over the radio. "We can see for mile and miles!"

Shane spoke. "Tony . . . let me see that thing."

Tony gave the radio to Shane, and Shane raised it to his lips. "Okay Holly, listen up. Do you think you guys can make it back to this side of the lake? Can you cut into the wind enough to make it back?"

There was a long pause, and finally, the radio crackled.

"Lyle says maybe," Holly answered. "But the wind is pretty strong. Right now, we seem to be in a spot where it isn't gusting, and we're just riding the currents."

Shane thought for a moment. Suddenly, his eyes lit up.

He keyed the microphone.

"Holly! Can you see Massasauga Swamp?"

The radio was silent for a moment, and for the first time, I noticed the goings-on around us. A few adults were sitting at picnic tables, sipping lemonade, chatting or reading books. Children played on the small, sandy beach, and some were swimming in the blue waters. The air was filled with the aroma of barbeques and suntan oil. It was a perfect August day in Great Bear Heart.

Except, high in the sky, disaster loomed.

"Yes," Holly's voice echoed from the radio. "Yes, we can see Massasauga Swamp fine from up here."

"Okay," Shane said into the radio. "Here's the plan. You're going to put the *Falcon* down in the swamp."

"What?!?!" Tony Gritter contested loudly. "Are you totally *nuts?!?!?"*

The radio sputtered to life. *"Are you crazy?"* came Holly O'Mara's surprised voice.

Dylan looked at Shane and spoke. "You've lost your marbles," he stated, eyes wide. Even I thought that Shane had a couple of screws loose.

Massasauga Swamp, on the outskirts of town, was named after one thing—Massasauga rattlesnakes. They are the only kind of rattlesnake we have in the state, and you usually don't see them much. They grow to about two feet long, and have dark brown or black blotches on their backs, with smaller blotches on their sides.

And they're *poisonous*.

But the real 'secret' about the swamp is this: there aren't any rattlesnakes in Massasauga Swamp! I've never seen one, and I've lived in Great Bear Heart all of my life. Plus, all of us in the Adventure Club have been through the swamp dozens of times. My dad says that, years ago, a man owned the entire marsh. To keep people out, he decided to call it 'Massasauga Swamp' in hopes that people would think it was infested with poisonous snakes. For the most part, his plan worked, as we've never come across any other people in the swamp . . . but we haven't come across any rattlesnakes, either. The fact is, there are simply no rattlesnakes in Massasauga Swamp.

"Shane," I asked, "how on earth are they going to land the *Falcon* in Massasauga Swamp? It's just a bunch of muck!"

"Parker," Shane answered, "we have a *big* problem here. A *BIG* problem." He pointed to the dot high in the sky, looked at me, then turned his gaze skyward. "That aircraft, for all practical purposes, is out of control. There's no way Lyle can put her down safely in this wind. Besides . . . you heard Lyle. The *Falcon* is damaged. She's not going to be able to stay in the sky much longer, and we've got to get Lyle and Holly down, somehow."

"But in Massasauga Swamp?!?!" I exclaimed.

Shane nodded. "Massasauga Swamp is huge. It's huge, and it's filled with mud. Sure, the landing won't be the prettiest thing . . . but there's nowhere else for them to land. At least the swamp is a big target, there are no trees or power lines, and landing in the mud will be a lot softer than hard-packed ground."

He didn't need to explain further. The *Falcon* was coming down—one way or another. Massasauga Swamp seemed like it would be Holly and Lyle's only chance.

Shane put the radio to his lips. "Holly . . . here's the plan. Listen carefully . . . ."

8

Twenty minutes later, Shane Mitchell, Tony Gritter, Dylan Bunker and I had ditched our bikes by the highway, and raced on foot down the trail that led back to Massasauga Swamp. The path was too overgrown with brush to ride our bicycles, and the trees grew too close to the trail. My pounding heart matched my drumming feet as we twisted and turned through the dense forest.

High above, Lyle had managed to keep control of the craft enough to steer it back from the lake and head north toward the swamp. We couldn't see the *Falcon* through the dense branches, but Holly was checking in over the radio every few seconds, letting us know that she and Lyle were okay.

So far, so good.

The trail wound through thick cedars, finally opening up at the mouth of the swamp. We stopped at the edge.

Massasauga Swamp is a lowland area. The ground is muddy and soft, and, in some places, there are pools of water teeming with cattails. Tall, sinewy grass grows all along the edges of the swamp. The air smells thick and damp, and is heavy with the scent of pine and cedar trees.

"Can you see us?" Shane spoke into the radio. We were looking up into the sky, watching the craft approach.

"Yeah, we see you," Holly's voice crackled from the tiny speaker.

"Okay, here's what you do," Shane instructed. "Bring the *Falcon* in high above the trees at the east end of the swamp. Give yourself a lot of distance over and between the branches, in case you get caught up in another gust of wind. Then, just aim for the swamp, nose first. Pull up at the last minute, and coast down into the mud. We'll be here if anything happens."

"Easy for you to say," Holly replied flatly over the radio. "You're down there, and we're up here."

We watched the tiny craft as it drew near, and my heart pounded like crazy. I was nervous, fearful, hopeful, and anxious. I had butterflies the size of blue jays flapping around in my stomach. In my pocket, I crossed my fingers, hoping for the best.

As the *Falcon* descended, the wind really tossed it around. The single wing acted like a trampoline, jerking the cockpit and its two occupants every which-way. Twice, we thought that Lyle had lost all control—once when the *Falcon* suddenly shot to the left, and again when it unexpectedly dropped like a rock for a few seconds. Our hearts were on a roller coaster ride as the experimental aircraft came in for a landing.

Suddenly, another gust of wind seized the plane, sending it lurching right toward the trees! It was going to crash!

My heart fell into my shoes.

"PULL UP! PULL UP! PULL UP!" Shane shouted into the radio. The four of us cringed, waiting for the worst.

At the edge of the swamp, the *Falcon* literally clipped the treetops, and we saw Lyle and Holly raise their legs as the small plane barely made it over the branches. That had been a close one!

The aircraft took another short, steep dive, and then leveled out again. We could see Lyle Haywood manning the controls. Holly O'Mara was clinging tightly to the radio with one hand, the edge of her seat with the other.

Lyle made some adjustments as another breeze caught the *Falcon,* sending it careening sideways. He had anticipated the gust, and was able to ride it out, but the craft was still high in the air. It skirted dangerously close to the treetops as it approached the swamp. One more heavy gust would spell disaster.

Please, wind, I thought. *Just a break. Just one break, please.*

As if it heard me, there was a sudden decrease in the wind. The craft stopped bouncing, and it leveled off as it continued its descent. Holly and Lyle were on track for a perfect landing. Of course, the muck and goo of the swamp was going to make the return to earth a bit more erratic, but that would be okay.

The *Falcon* continued to glide effortlessly over the marsh, and the four of us on the ground breathed a bit easier. As it descended below the tree line, the plane was no longer directly in the wind. Holly and Lyle looked more relaxed, and we could even see Lyle smiling as the plane passed us by, about twenty feet overhead. We cheered, shouting words of encouragement.

"Way to go!" Tony Gritter yelled.

"Yeah!" I chimed. "Bring'er on home!"

The small craft was gently floating to the earth, and was about to make as good of a landing as it possibly could in a swamp.

But it was not to be.

To our horror, the damaged wing bolt finally broke,

sending the small plane straight down in a free-fall, into the swamp below.

9

We had thought the plane was going to make it. I'm sure that Lyle and Holly thought the same thing, too.

Suddenly, there was a loud, terrible *snap!* and the cockpit nearly tore away from the wing canopy. The result was a crippled wing dangling above a hobbled cockpit, and both large pieces plunged straight toward the ground.

There was no doubt about it this time. The *Falcon* was going to crash.

Lyle and Holly were screaming. Dylan Bunker was screaming. I don't think I was screaming, but I could have been. The blue jays in my stomach had flown up to my throat, and I almost choked to death trying to keep them in.

The entire apparatus—cockpit, wing, and occupants—came crashing down into the muck-filled swamp.

Aluminum and metal clanked together. Wires snapped. There was a single, heavy *crunch!* as the *Falcon* slammed into the earth.

Shane sprang from the dry embankment where we were standing and immediately began trudging through the grimy, thick goo, heading for the crash site. I followed, and so did Tony, and then Dylan Bunker plunged in. We sank up to our knees in syrup-like muck.

In the middle of the swamp, the doomed craft lay in a jumbled, disheveled pile. There was no movement, no signs of life from around or beneath the wreckage.

We were frantic. The knee-deep goo sucked at our shoes, making it almost impossible to walk. I lost one of my sneakers, and so did Tony.

But we pressed on.

"Holly! Lyle!" we hollered out. "Holly! Lyle!"

We forged through the swamp. The deep muck made for some tough-going, but we were relentless.

As we approached the crashed aircraft, our anxiety grew. We'd had a lot of adventures over the summer, and we'd been pretty lucky—so far.

Suddenly, we saw movement. A dirty, wet arm appeared over the torn wing of the plane.

It was Holly!

"Hang on!" I shouted, struggling to move through the

thick, cement-like goop. "We're almost there!"

After a few more gooey, mud-soaked steps, we were at the crash site. I grasped one part of the single wing, Dylan grabbed the other, and we lifted with all of our strength. An entire section had plunged deep into the muck, and it was really hard to budge it. Finally, after more frantic struggling, we succeeded in pulling the canopy away from the wreck.

Holly stood up immediately. She was covered in mud from her head to her toe. There wasn't one spot on her that wasn't stained by dark, brown goo . . . except when she took her helmet off. Most of her head and her hair remained mud-free, and, except for a few scratches, she was all right.

"Lyle!" Shane shouted. "You okay?!?" Lyle was still strapped in the cockpit, which had been driven sideways in the mud.

"I . . . I think so," he said, struggling to release his seat belt. Sticky mud splashed as he battled with the nylon strap. Tony reached down and helped release Lyle from the safety belt, then helped him stand up.

"Are you all right?" I asked.

"Yeah, I think I'm fine," he replied, reaching down to wipe away the mud on his legs. "I really am."

"Man . . . that was some pretty fancy flying," Shane

said, congratulating Lyle. He offered his hand, and Lyle shook it. "And you made a great co-pilot," Shane commended, pulling his hand from Lyle and extending it to Holly. She grasped his hand, and Holly smirked.

"Next time, it will be *you* up there," she smiled, pointing a convicting finger at Shane Mitchell.

"I don't think there will be a next time," Lyle speculated, wiping a hunk of mud away from his eyes. "From this point on, I think we should keep all of our adventures on the ground. And above ground. And out of the water. And the cemetery."

We broke out laughing, for we all knew what he had meant. We'd had some pretty fun times this past summer—playing that joke on Norm Beeblemeyer, rebuilding the old sub, exploring what was behind the hidden door, and discovering the old graveyard. And we'd had some close calls,

But man . . . what a fun summer it had been! Every day held the promise of something new and fun.

I reached down, dug up a handful of mud, and slapped Lyle Haywood on the back. "Good flying!" I exclaimed. Lyle laughed, and bent down. He reached into the muck and grabbed a handful of goop.

"Good guidance!" he replied, smearing the brown gunk all over the front of my shirt. Shane got into the act, then

Tony, then Dylan and Holly. It was hysterical. Soon, we were all covered, from head to toe, in dark, syrup-like muck.

And, amid the flying sludge, we laughed until our sides hurt. It had been a fun summer . . . the kind of summer you never forget. As I hurled mud at my friends, and they threw it back at me, I remembered what my dad had told me earlier in the year. He said to make sure that every day counts, because soon, they're going to fade away. Soon, Dad said, our club wouldn't be able to get together once a week and have the kind of adventures we were having. In time, he said, we'd all be grown-ups, and have our own families and jobs and responsibilities and bills to pay, and all that. Our priorities would change, he said, and life would be very different than it is today. He said I would change when I grew older, that we all would change. Our Adventure Club would be something we would look back on and smile—and that the club wouldn't last forever.

And maybe Dad was right.

But all of that would come later. Right now, I had five great friends—friends that you just don't find anywhere.

I picked up another handful of the blackest, gooiest muck I could find, splattered it all over Tony Gritter's back, and time seemed to stop. I thought about my friends—Lyle Haywood, probably one of the smartest people I've ever met. Shane Mitchell, who, even in the scariest situations, could take charge and be a real leader. Holly O'Mara, who was, I must admit, very pretty. She was also smarter than smart, and a very kind person, too. Tony Gritter—the prankster of the group—could be kind of tough and brassy, but he was always there for you when you needed him. *Always*. And Dylan Bunker, who, even though he was kind of klutzy, had a big heart, and he cared a lot about everyone. Dylan Bunker was always fifteen minutes late for everything . . . but as a true friend, he had perfect timing.

And on this particular hot August afternoon, knee-deep in mud in the middle of Massasauga Swamp, laughing and whooping it up, I considered myself luckier than lucky. With friends like Shane, Tony, Lyle, Holly, and Dylan, I knew I was the luckiest person in the world. At that very second, I didn't think our adventures could be any more fun than they already had been.

That is, of course, until the day Holly and I found two silver dollars in an abandoned shed over on Oak street.

Two *old* silver dollars . . . just like Dylan Bunker had found in the tunnel beneath the library.

The hunt for the chest of stolen coins was about to begin—but that, my friends, is another story altogether.

ABOUT THE AUTHOR

Johnathan Rand is the author of more than 65 books, with well over 4 million copies in print. Series include **AMERICAN CHILLERS, MICHIGAN CHILLERS, FREDDIE FERNORTNER, FEARLESS FIRST GRADER**, and **THE ADVENTURE CLUB.** He's also co-authored a novel for teens (with Christopher Knight) entitled **PANDEMIA**. When not traveling, Rand lives in northern Michigan with his wife and three dogs. He is also the only author in the world to have a store that sells only his works: **CHILLERMANIA!** is located in Indian River, Michigan. Johnathan Rand is not always at the store, but he has been known to drop by frequently. Find out more at:

www.americanchillers.com

EXIT

www.americanchillers.com

Other books by Johnathan Rand:

Michigan Chillers:

#1: Mayhem on Mackinac Island
#2: Terror Stalks Traverse City
#3: Poltergeists of Petoskey
#4: Aliens Attack Alpena
#5: Gargoyles of Gaylord
#6: Strange Spirits of St. Ignace
#7: Kreepy Klowns of Kalamazoo
#8: Dinosaurs Destroy Detroit
#9: Sinister Spiders of Saginaw
#10: Mackinaw City Mummies
#11: Great Lakes Ghost Ship
#12: AuSable Alligators
#13: Gruesome Ghouls of Grand Rapids
#14: Bionic Bats of Bay City

American Chillers:

#1: The Michigan Mega-Monsters
#2: Ogres of Ohio
#3: Florida Fog Phantoms
#4: New York Ninjas
#5: Terrible Tractors of Texas
#6: Invisible Iguanas of Illinois
#7: Wisconsin Werewolves
#8: Minnesota Mall Mannequins
#9: Iron Insects Invade Indiana
#10: Missouri Madhouse
#11: Poisonous Pythons Paralyze Pennsylvania
#12: Dangerous Dolls of Delaware
#13: Virtual Vampires of Vermont
#14: Creepy Condors of California
#15: Nebraska Nightcrawlers
#16: Alien Androids Assault Arizona
#17: South Carolina Sea Creatures
#18: Washington Wax Museum
#19: North Dakota Night Dragons
#20: Mutant Mammoths of Montana
#21: Terrifying Toys of Tennessee
#22: Nuclear Jellyfish of New Jersey
#23: Wicked Velociraptors of West Virginia
#24: Haunting in New Hampshire
#25: Mississippi Megalodon
#26: Oklahoma Outbreak
#27: Kentucky Komodo Dragons
#28: Curse of the Connecticut Coyotes

Freddie Fernortner, Fearless First Grader:

#1: The Fantastic Flying Bicycle
#2: The Super-Scary Night Thingy
#3: A Haunting We Will Go
#4: Freddie's Dog Walking Service
#5: The Big Box Fort
#6: Mr. Chewy's Big Adventure
#7: The Magical Wading Pool
#8: Chipper's Crazy Carnival
#9: Attack of the Dust Bunnies from Outer Space!
#10: The Pond Monster

Adventure Club series:

#1: Ghost in the Graveyard
#2: Ghost in the Grand
#3: The Haunted Schoolhouse

For Teens:

PANDEMIA: A novel of the bird flu and the end of the world
(written with Christopher Knight)

American Chillers Double Thrillers:

Vampire Nation & Attack of the Monster Venus Melon

All AudioCraft books are proudly printed, bound, and manufactured in the United States of America, utilizing American resources, labor, and materials.

USA